Outside In

Also by Jennifer Bradbury

A Moment Comes
River Runs Deep
Shift
Wrapped

Outside In

Jennifer Bradbury

A Caitlyn Dlouhy Book

Atheneum Books for Young Readers

New York London Toronto Sydney New Delhi

ATHENEUM BOOKS FOR YOUNG READERS

An imprint of Simon & Schuster Children's Publishing Division

1230 Avenue of the Americas, New York, New York 10020

This book is a work of fiction. Any references to historical events, real people, or real places are used fictitiously. Other names, characters, places, and events are products of the author's imagination, and any resemblance to actual events or places or persons, living or dead, is entirely coincidental.

Text copyright © 2017 by Jennifer Bradbury

Jacket illustration copyright © 2017 by John Jay Cabuay

All rights reserved, including the right of reproduction in whole or in part in any form.

ATHENEUM BOOKS FOR YOUNG READERS is a registered trademark of Simon & Schuster, Inc. Atheneum logo is a trademark of Simon & Schuster, Inc.

For information about special discounts for bulk purchases, please contact Simon & Schuster Special Sales at 1-866-506-1949 or business@simonandschuster.com.

The Simon & Schuster Speakers Bureau can bring authors to your live event. For more information or to book an event, contact the Simon & Schuster Speakers Bureau at 1-866-248-3049 or visit our website at www.simonspeakers.com.

Book design by Debra Sfetsios-Conover and Irene Metaxatos

The text for this book was set in ITC Berkeley Oldstyle.

Manufactured in the United States of America

0517 FFG

First Edition

10 9 8 7 6 5 4 3 2 1

CIP data for this book is available from the Library of Congress.

ISBN 978-1-4424-6827-6 (hc)

ISBN 978-1-4424-6829-0 (eBook)

To all who make
because they must

Outside In

"Once more." The big ugly one steps forward.

Ram knows this one is named Vijay, but to Ram he is Peach Fuzz, owing to the shadow of a mustache at his upper lip. He's bigger than he ought to be, compared to the pack he commands. Bigger than Ram certainly.

Ram weighs the money in his parcel. He's already got more money in there than he's ever held at one time.

He loves this time of year, the monthlong holiday season that starts with Dussehra and closes with Diwali. Others love the season for the parades and the days off from school or work, or the fireworks and pageants, the prayer services, the gatherings of family and friends. Ram loves it because *bewakoofs* like these always have extra pocket money on account of aunties and uncles sending them gifts.

Ram's beaten Peach Fuzz both other times they've played. He knows he can win. That's not what worries him. It's more the fact that every time he and Daya run into Peach Fuzz and his gang in the park, Daya reminds Ram that Peach Fuzz is the toughest kid in her school. Daya's only in fourth form, Peach Fuzz is in eighth. But according to Daya, even the eleventh and twelfth formers steer clear of him.

"You can't afford to lose to me again," Ram now tells him.

"One more," Peach Fuzz orders.

That's the thing about *gilli*. It's a simple game. All it requires is a thumb-size piece of wood—tapered on the ends—and a long stick to serve as a *danda*, or bat. The batter uses the *danda* to pop the *gilli* off the ground. Then, while the *gilli* spins in the air, the batter strikes it again with the *danda* to hit it as far as he can. It's a game everyone thinks they're good at because they've all played it dozens of times, either in teams at the park or the schoolyard, or on their own to practice hitting. But Ram has done it thousands of times more. And most always on his own, perfecting the flip and swing and strike of the batting motion while other kids are at school learning maths or at home having dinner with their families.

Of course, he never lets on how much practice he's had. So kids see his ratty clothes and his bare feet and his shaggy hair and figure they can take his money easily. But they never do.

Today was no different. Ram flipped up the *gilli* with his makeshift bat, and each time sent it farther than the boy who stepped up last to challenge him.

Tap. Flip. Swing. Crack.

Clink.

The pile of rupees grew in Ram's hand. But every time one of the boys paid up, the pack grew more restless and their glares at Ram and Daya darkened.

Peach Fuzz digs deep in his pocket and comes up with a few more coins. Ram is tempted, but the little extra isn't worth the risk of losing this bunch as a source of income. Ram's made that mistake before. The trick is always to quit when they still think they *can* beat you. So yes, he could take Peach Fuzz's last few coins, but he might never get money off him again.

"Besides," Peach Fuzz says, almost friendly, "I've figured out your trick."

"There's no trick," Daya says. "He's just better than all of you. Ram doesn't need tricks—"

"Not very sporting to not give me a chance to win back some of our money," Peach Fuzz says.

"Neither is being a sore loser," Daya shoots back, reaching for her school bag. "Let's go, Ram."

"Wait!" Peach Fuzz says. "What if I made it worth your while?" He pulls back his sleeve to reveal the fancy wristwatch Ram noticed before. It is a digital one, with lots of little buttons, an alarm that beeps, and even a little line with the day of the week and month. Ram *never* knows what day it is. Daya's father, Mr. Singh, has one just like this that Ram has envied before.

"I caught you admiring it earlier," Peach Fuzz says. "It's a good one. Totally waterproof. And the battery is supposed to last ten years. My mother's sister just sent it to me all the way from America."

Ram guesses the watch is worth a fortune, and even if it isn't, he'll likely never have a chance to own something so wonderful again.

Peach Fuzz knows he has Ram hooked. "You

beat me again, and this watch is yours. I beat you, you give back all our money."

"You're not getting your money back, Vijay," Daya says, "and you won't even give him the watch when he beats you."

Vijay pulls the watch off and offers it out to Daya. "You can hold it. Until after the batting. Good faith."

Daya looks at Ram. Ram knows he shouldn't. He can feel in his bones that this could end very badly. But he can also already feel the perfect weight of that fancy watch on his wrist.

He starts to pull his best *gilli* from the parcel.

"*Nahi*," Peach Fuzz says. "We're not using your good one. We always use that one. This time, *I'm* picking it."

It brings him luck, this *gilli*, but Ram doesn't need luck to beat Peach Fuzz. He passes the parcel to Daya.

Peach Fuzz grins wickedly. His gang whistles and hoots behind him.

A moment later Peach Fuzz comes up with a sorry excuse for a *gilli*, but it will do. Ram retrieves the stout branch they were using as *danda* earlier.

"You first," Ram says.

Peach Fuzz takes the *danda* and places the *gilli* on the ground.

He lines up the shot.

Tap. Flip. Swing. Crack.

The hit is good, better than Ram figured on. It sails a good five meters into the grass, halfway to the exercise path where an old uncle on a three-wheeled cycle is making slow circles.

But Ram isn't worried.

Peach Fuzz and one of his boys walk out to fetch the *gilli*. Peach Fuzz stands on the spot it fell to mark it and sends his minion back to Ram with the *gilli*.

Ram doesn't hesitate. He can't resist showing off. He drops, hits, and sends the *gilli* flying with alarming speed. It sails over Peach Fuzz's head, landing on the cycle track beyond.

Ram drops the bat. He glances at Peach Fuzz and sees the shock on his face, thinks how the boy looks like a stupid tree planted out of place in the middle of the pitch. Another glance at the rest of the boys and Ram can see they're all unsure what to do.

He figures it is time to go. Daya has had the same thought. She's already halfway to the edge of the park. He jogs to catch up to her. And even though she is sensible enough to get some distance, she isn't sensible enough to resist the urge to launch one final taunt.

"Better luck next *time*," she shouts with too much glee as she waggles the watch in the air over her head.

"Daya!" Ram warns her as he collects the bag and watch.

But Daya can't stop. "By the way, did you know it only took you thirty-six seconds to lose this fancy watch? I timed you."

"*Daya*—"

"Get them!" Peach Fuzz shouts.

Ram and Daya break into a run. At least they have a head start.

They rocket across the road, diving into the crowd of pedestrians streaming up the sidewalk. It is only a few hundred meters back to their sector. This walk is usually one of Ram's favorites. All the nicer restaurants in Chandigarh flank this street. Ram often walks extra slow along here just to linger in the good smells of meat roasting in the tandoors, the spicy tang of tamarind, and the slow-simmering creamy *dal makhani*.

He bumps into a woman wandering the street

selling fresh marigold garlands; a dozen chains of brilliant orange flowers drape over her neck like an exotic shawl.

"Sorry, auntie!" He pauses long enough to return the fallen ones to her hands and hurries to catch up to Daya.

"Why did you stop?" Daya puffs, her school bag bouncing against her back.

"Just keep running! We'll make it!"

They skirt the next roundabout, barely pausing at the corner before plunging into the street. An auto rickshaw horn blares at them. A cyclist swerves, drops his foot to the pavement, and curses at Ram and Daya as they reach the other corner.

He thinks of the old man on the bicycle back at the park, thinks again how much easier a bicycle would make escapes like this one.

Another coordinated chorus of horns and shouting drivers tells Ram that the pack has lost a little ground on him and Daya.

Good.

Ram is quick. Plus, he's not wrapped up in a school blazer and tie and long pants or even wearing shoes to slow him down. But Daya wears her starchy uniform, stiff shoes like the other boys. She's fast enough, but not as fast as Ram on his own.

He urges her on. "Almost there!"

They round the back corner of the sector occupied by the bicycle factory. In the far distance the foothills leading up to Kasauli and Shimla hover on the horizon. Ram loves this time of year in the Punjab, when the air cools and the haze disappears and the mountains return like forgotten old friends. He loves the brilliant red and gold of the trees that line the wide avenues. He loves his city all scrubbed and illuminated for the festivals. He loves it all even though he knows it also means the cold is coming, and months of shivering through the night await him.

Daya's father's building looms halfway up the street on the right. Barely breaking stride, Ram reaches into his pocket and fishes out the small packet Mr. Singh sent Ram to fetch from the post office. "Give this to your father!"

"Don't forget my commission!" she says. "Five percent!" Daya peels off toward the square municipal building with its grooved concrete and dark windows.

"Three!" Ram says, running on, though they

both know Daya has to work out the numbers for him anyway.

Daya bounds up the steps to the front door two at a time. The doorman sees her coming, shuts the door quickly behind her. Then he glares at Ram, shaking his head. All this before the boys round the corner at the end of the street. They've not seen Daya disappear. She at least is safe.

And soon Ram will be too. He shoves the watch in his pocket and lets loose, uncorking the speed he's been holding back to stay with Daya. He's near enough now to make it home, near enough to—

But then he pitches forward, one toe catching on an uneven seam in the concrete. His arms spin as he fights to stay on his feet and his parcel swings up and away. Even though his brain screams at his hand to hold on to the knot, his grip fails. He watches with horror as his bag sails through the iron bars that make up the gate to the bicycle factory.

Splat. Ram twists and lands on his shoulder in a pile of what he hopes is only mud, but he expects all the luck he awoke with today has already been used up. His parcel lands next to the back wheel of a bicycle leaning against a tree. The gate guard doesn't seem to have noticed.

Ram scrambles to his feet.

He could climb the gate and get his parcel. Or he could beg the guard to get it for him.

But both would take too much time.

Ram glances back. Maybe fifty meters away, the pack of boys—a tangle of stupid blue coats, faces as red as the ties they wear—breaks around the corner. From here, they look like one body with ten heads and twenty arms.

Twenty arms could do a lot of damage.

It hurts him to do so, but Ram leaves the bag; he can figure out a way to get it later after the boys have grown bored and given up. So before he is spotted, Ram bolts across the road, arrows into his alley, and disappears.

Ram found the alley last spring, when the rains came and his old spot in the park flooded. Formed by the buildings on either side, the alley was narrow enough to keep the rain from sheeting inside.

When the rain had let up enough for him to explore, he found he could climb onto the roof of one of the buildings. The roof had a low wall along its perimeter, and a big painted wooden sign mounted to the wall facing the street. The sign had been braced by lumber angled from the flat roof to the back of the sign, and then covered with a few sheets of corrugated metal to keep water from collecting around the base. The space was long enough that if he crawled into the middle, he could stretch out and sleep and stay mostly dry.

The storefront below him belongs to a dance school. Ram has not seen much of the dancing, but the music plays all hours of the day and covers the noise of his thumping around on the roof. For that he is grateful, though the beat of the *banghra* sometimes rattles his teeth.

Now Ram crouches next to his sleeping spot, scanning the street. He pulls the watch from his pocket, buckles it on his wrist. *It was worth it,* he thinks, *to have something so wonderful.* He fiddles with the buttons, delighted at the little chirping noises the watch produces. When he has more time, he'll figure out how to operate the timer like Daya did.

He tears his eyes away from the fancy watch to look out across the four lanes of traffic below. The Hero Bicycle factory with its tall brick enclosure occupies the better part of the sector it lies in. His bag is still there. Then he scans up the road in both directions. No sign of a blue blazer or a red tie. Good. But Ram will wait another few minutes to be sure the boys are truly good and gone, and to figure out how to talk his way past the guard at the gate of the factory.

At the south corner of the sector, the little shrine overflows. The pickings are always good this time of year as the festivals come on. Someone cleaned the shrine and repainted the clothes of the figures recently. There are garlands of fresh marigolds draped over the stone arch. Beneath the arch, four painted ceramic figures pose like dolls in a toy-shop window. The first is a blue-skinned man holding a fearsome bow, an arrow set in the notch. Ram knows his name because he once asked a kind old woman leaving a bowl of rice at the shrine who he was. "Lord Rama, child," she answered, sounding as if she couldn't believe he'd asked such a question.

Rama! he'd thought delightedly. So close to his own name. He wanted to know more about the blue-skinned man and his friends, but the woman moved on and the statues remained as mysterious as his own name. A name he could just barely remember being called as a little boy. The girl had called him that before she went away. Now he rubs the clay bead on the red cord inside his shirt like a talisman. When he tries to conjure up her face, he muddles it with that of the beautiful lady standing next to Lord Rama under the arch, the second of the four ceramic figures.

The third figure, another man, stands behind them, his face grim, skin darker. Ram can never decide if he's about to attack blue-skinned Rama or if he's protecting him. And at the feet of the blue-skinned man kneels a figure with the body of a man but the face and tail of a monkey.

When he dared ask others about the figurines, they ignored him, mumbled about how disgraceful it was that the city was *already* so full of beggars.

Ram hasn't begged for years. He earns his money well enough hitting *gilli*, even if it does mean he has to outrun some angry opponents now and then. Still, the sidewalk in front of the shrine is full of good things Ram can pilfer for his supper. Little clay bowls of rice, juicy red apples, maybe even a box of sweets—

The factory whistle cuts short his imaginary feast.

Siyappa! Is it really so late?

But the guard is already opening the iron gate, shoving it along like a stubborn cow.

Supper will have to wait.

R am crawls out of his hiding place, runs across the rooftop, jumps to a corrugated metal awning over the back door, and then swings down to the alley.

When he gets to the street, he's relieved to see his parcel remains where it fell against the rear tire of the bicycle. But a man, a factory worker, approaches.

The man is short, shoulders curled forward as he walks, eyes blank as he makes his way to the bicycle. He is sad, Ram decides, or maybe just bored from a whole day spent fitting chains around gears on new bicycles. His dark hair is in need of a trim, but not as desperately as Ram's own shaggy black curls. The man's gray cotton tunic and pants are smeared with grease. Another worker calls to him as he comes up to the bicycle, but the man is so distracted that the worker friend shouts louder. "Hey, Nek!"

But that's all Ram hears above the sudden noise of the traffic in the street. The other man nods and walks away. The one called Nek loads a shiny metal tiffin box into the crate mounted on the back of the bicycle.

Good, thinks Ram, *stay distracted. Just ride away and I can fetch my bag.*

Instead Nek bends down to roll up the cuffs of his trousers to keep them from tangling in the bike chain. Then his hands go still around his ankle. He reaches over and picks up Ram's parcel.

Oh teri deri! Ram's hands go to his forehead, his hair, to grab two fistfuls of it. *No!*

Nek straightens. He tests the weight of the bag.

Ram cannot breathe. There is enough money in that bundle for him to eat well for a month. He stands horrified as Nek calls out to the other worker who just spoke to him, gesturing at the parcel. That man shrugs and exits the gate.

Nek faces the guard, holds up Ram's bag, the question written in his eyes.

The guard tilts his head to one side, waves lazily.

Nek holds the bag in his palm like an offering. After a beat, he drops the bag into the crate and takes the bicycle by the handlebars.

Ram is already moving, already scheming how best to get his parcel back. Simplest would be asking, explaining what happened. But people don't listen to boys like Ram. Singh does, but nobody else really. Nobody believes a street kid comes by that much money honestly.

No. The smartest thing to do is wait until this Nek fellow stops. Then Ram can rush the bike from behind, pinch the parcel from the crate, and melt into the crowd. Nek doesn't mount the bicycle when he clears the wall surrounding the factory. Good. A little more time.

Ram begins his approach, careful to keep out of the man's eye line.

Nek pauses at the shrine at the corner. He leans the bicycle against his leg and pulls the parcel from the crate. Ram leans back against the brick factory wall and watches from the corner of his eye.

The man jiggles the bag, and Ram is close enough to hear all those lovely rupee coins jingling. Nek unties the knot.

That's mine! Ram screams inwardly. *Stop!*

Nek's fingers rake through the contents. Ram knows well what hides inside. His best *gilli* stick. A few *parathas* and an apple he saved from this morning's breakfast. And all those coins. The man scoots the coins around, counting them with one finger.

Then Nek plucks out what looks to be at least one-fourth of the afternoon's winnings. He stacks the coins in the little space at the foot of the shrine. Then he reties the knot and returns the parcel to the crate. Before he goes, Nek flattens his palms against each other, lifts his hands to his forehead, and bows, the bike slipping down his leg.

Finally, he yanks the bicycle upright, mounts, and pedals away.

Ram dashes to snatch up the coins, grabbing a mango while he's at it, hoping no one is watching. He starts to move off, but the gaze of the blue man inside the shrine follows him eerily. Ram does his best to bow the way the factory man just did before he breaks into a jog.

It seems unfair to have had to run away after earning this money only to have to chase it down again now. But he learned long ago that fair is for those boys with their blue coats and red ties. Not him.

Following Nek is easier than Ram anticipated. Even though the man is on a bicycle, the lanes are crowded and he has to stop often for traffic signals and crossings. Ram has plenty of time to eat the mango. It is just shy of being fully ripe, so it makes his mouth itchy, but he tosses the pit aside after six giant bites and wipes the sticky juice on the hem of his shirt.

The city is easy to navigate—all the lanes as straight as compass needles, fat roundabouts planted at their intersections. Chandigarh is a young city, still growing. Singh—who helps build and plan the roads and the sectors that lie between them—told Ram that Chandigarh was built as a symbol of hope and new beginnings after all the terrible things that happened during Partition. Partition, Singh explained, meant to separate into parts. Like peeling and dividing an orange into sections. Only in this case, it meant separating India into two countries—Pakistan in the north and India to the south. Partition was supposed to make things more peaceful, allowing people to choose which side they wanted to live on. But many were hurt or killed or lost in the messy business of making two countries out of one.

Ram has overheard old men in the park swapping tales, comparing accounts of the horrors that they or their families suffered during the division of lands and villages. Those same old storytellers now worry about what might happen next between India and Pakistan, about more trouble along the borders.

Ram can't fathom how a new city can fix such troubles, but Singh seems to believe that it has helped. A new beginning for a new chapter in India, he calls it. Singh claims there is no place like it in all of India or Pakistan. An island of peace and progress, with wide streets built on a perfect grid, the sectors meant to be self-contained, each with its own school, shopping complex, temples. Ram likes the order, likes how the arrow-straight roads have two lanes going both directions, and walking and cycling paths at their margins, strips of greenery in the middles, studded with trees now going gold and red with the coming of the winter. At the edges of the streets rise up brick walls, some two or three meters high. Behind the walls sit houses, apartment buildings, office buildings, and schools. Singh once told Ram that the city won't allow buildings taller than nine floors, and since then, Ram has made it a game to try to find one with a tenth. So far he hasn't. The shapes of the buildings echo the same block pattern of the streets themselves, but with little touches to make them unique: a wall painted in a soothing blue, or a curved iron gate offering a peek at a front garden.

Ram loves Chandigarh, but someday he'll travel to other cities. Someday he'll earn enough money to buy a bicycle. And then he can earn enough to buy his own rickshaw, and then a *tuk-tuk*, and maybe even one day a taxi. Then he'll drive all over India, maybe even drive far enough to find the girl who left him behind.

Ram needs that money. This Nek doesn't. He's even given some away at the shrine like it doesn't matter at all! Ram fumes at the thought that the fortune he worked so hard for has ended up with this fool.

Ram knows this route, though he's used it only a couple of times to go back and forth to the lake at the edge of town. Knowing the way makes it easy to follow at a distance, and easier still because the man stops often to dig through piles of trash, or to pick up an old burlap bag that has been flattened and molded itself to the surface of the road. He adds things to the crate mounted to his bicycle and rides on. As they near the edge of the city, when the lights begin to fade and the noise is only a rumble instead of a roar, the proper road ends. Even here there are signs that the city is growing. Tools—shovels, picks, and wheelbarrows—wait for workmen to reclaim them in the morning. And all around are the stones that the workers have dug up in the quest to lay out the new streets. Some are piled in crude pyramids; others wait in line by the side of the someday street. Across the unfinished road stands a riot of trees and vines and too-tall grass—a tract of uncleared forest that marks the edge of the planned city. According to Singh, some-day all those trees will be cleared out to make way for more sectors as the city grows.

Nek leans his bicycle up against a great steel bar-rel and studies the stones. The light is almost gone now. Ram hides behind a bus stand as the man picks up stone after stone, struggling with some that are as big as pumpkins. The man tests them; he rolls them around on the trenched-up earth to check their shapes and edges, staring at one for a few seconds before nodding to himself and adding it to the crate. Then he goes back for another.

Ram can understand that the man would take his parcel and his money, but rocks? Trash from the street? He must be mad.

When the crate is full and Nek has repositioned the smaller items around the stones he has col-lected, he climbs back on the bicycle. The heavy load strains the frame, and the tires ride low in the rear. Nek pedals slowly, the extra weight straining him as well.

It would be simple to run him down now, but the road is empty and Nek will see him coming.

Half a mile beyond where the road construction ends, the forest grows even denser. And here Nek dismounts and wheels his bicycle right into its heart. Ram can just make out the man's tunic as he unloads something from the crate and disappears into the trees.

Perfect. Ram runs to the bicycle, peers into the crate.

No bag.

Siyappa. The man must have taken it with him.

Perhaps he has a hiding place back in these trees. Ram has to hope so. He needs that money. And his *gilli* stick. It's his lucky one. The one the girl taught him to play with all those years ago. Since then, the edges have been honed away, and Ram knows that no matter how it spins, he can hit it true.

Ram avoids the path the man has worn into the forest floor, and presses through the curtain of vines, his arm brushing the fuzzy undersides of a curry-leaf shrub, sending up a nutty, spicy smell he recognizes from the market stalls. Ram startles at the warning bark of a langur, sees the monkey's white tail and black hands and feet land on a thick branch before springing off again. He's seen monkeys pestering people in town. They're funny there. An annoyance as they snitch food or overturn rubbish bins. But out here, in the forest, this one seems wild, and it makes Ram's heart pound to see it disappear.

A few minutes later, he is startled to see Nek returning to his bicycle. Ram melts behind a tree, going still as Nek passes. He counts to twenty, then moves as fast as he can in the direction Nek came from, taking the trail this time. He'll find his parcel and be gone before Nek is even aware that he's been followed.

A hundred meters farther, Ram stumbles into ring of rounded stones framing a clearing about three meters wide. Inside the ring, two low fires—freshly lit, judging by the smoke—burn on rough metal squares. Bicycle tires, Ram realizes. The man is burning bicycle tires, maybe even ones from the factory where he works. They produce just enough light to hold back the twilight and the shadows of the trees.

A tarp, its corners affixed to four stout trees with thin cord, shelters an assortment of junk. Buckets, wooden kegs, something that might be a pile of sticks, bag after lumpy bag filled with who knows what. Piles of broken glass, the colors shining back under the blue-orange flames, heaps of rags, scraps of cloth, a few odd dishes and flowerpots. In front of the tarp is a stool, and beside the stool the squat figure of a statue—half Ram's height, the arms too long for the body.

But nowhere is Ram's parcel.

What is this place? Ram's fear begins to crowd out his wonder. The clearing is a like a nest. A hidden place. Or possibly a trap.

Then Ram hears footsteps crunching on the narrow track. Nek is coming. And Ram hasn't found his money.

But he knows he can't leave without it.

Ram shimmies up a ropy banyan tree, settles into a wide branch, bracing his feet against the main trunk. The smoke is stronger up here, and it dawns on Ram that the fires might be for more than just light. The flames and smoke could also be for keeping animals—particularly snakes—at bay.

Snakes. Ram shivers. Of course there are snakes. How could Ram not have thought of snakes before? How many could be waiting between where he sits now and the road a hundred meters away? How many might hide in the branches above him, even? He's almost spooked enough to run, but then Nek

reappears, struggling with one of the stones he collected by the road.

Ram is torn. He twists the bead on the cord he
wears around his neck, considering his options.
Should he go? Come back at daylight and search for
his money? But Nek might just as easily take it with
him to wherever he lives. And then what will Ram
do? No. Snakes or not, Ram is not leaving without
that money.

Nek places the rock carefully—as if it is a great,
delicate egg—into the ring that forms the perimeter
of the clearing. Then he scans the little work area,
studying the dusty ground. *Footprints?* Ram worries
as he, too, scans the earth. *Did I leave footprints?*
Nek peers into the forest, and Ram holds his breath,
afraid now he is not high enough to avoid being
seen, despite the dark.

After too long, Nek scratches the top of his head,
then shrugs and settles on the little stool by the
funny statue.

Ram can hear him murmuring.

"How are you this evening, friend?"

What?

"Yes, I believe you are almost ready to join the
others."

Others? Then Ram understands that the man is talking to the statue. He's mystified and more than a little uneasy at being alone in the dark with this strange man who has stolen his fortune. A thief who collects junk and apparently talks to statues.

And Ram can't forget about the snakes, no matter how much he'd like to.

But his money . . .

Nek fetches a tin pail and a large glass jar from beneath the tarp. He lays these beside the statue. Unrolling the top of one of the heavy paper bags Ram saw earlier, he tips it into the pail. A fine gray powder streams out, dust puffing up like Ram's breath does on the cold mornings he's been waking up to lately. Nek pours a measure of water from the jar, and then stirs water and powder together with a long stick, the sides of the bucket clank dully as he mixes.

"Yes, I see the mortar is too thick," Nek says to the statue. "Patience." He trickles more water from the jar, stirs again. Then he holds it up to the statue man. "*Han?*"

The man is *pagal*, Ram is sure of it.

Nek leaves the bucket at the feet of the statue, and then shuffles back under the tarp. The pile of junk shifts and clanks as the man digs through it.

Nek emerges at last with a glazed clay pot. Even in the firelight, Ram can see how bright the colors are, how shiny the glaze. A great crack splits the side from the rim to an inch or so above the base. Broken. Ram is surprised that it even still holds together.

But then Nek does something even more surprising. He lays the pot on the ground upside down, palms a rock in his fist, and brings it down hard on the bottom. The pot spreads out like a pressed flower. Then Nek flips each piece over, hits it a few more times with his rock until a pile of littler pieces waits at his feet.

Picking up one, he reaches into the bucket and scoops up some of the mortar with a tablespoon, buttering the back of the shard before sticking it carefully onto the body of the statue.

"Hush," Nek says. "Your armor may be prettier than the others. But no one likes a boaster."

The man is mad, but Ram is mesmerized as Nek covers the body of the figure in scales broken from the pot. Dip into the bucket with the spoon, fetch up a shard from the pile at his feet, swipe the spoon across the back, and then puzzle the piece into place on the body of the statue. When a few dozen pieces have been placed, Nek sighs loudly.

"You are quiet tonight, my friend."

Ram holds himself very, very still.

"Since you are so silent, shall I tell you a secret?"

Ram can't resist a secret, no matter what it is, whether it has anything to do with him or not. Can't resist it even if the teller might be crazy. Or dangerous.

The man leans close, his voice dropping low. "Nek can trust you, yes?"

Nek waits for the stone face to respond, but when it doesn't, he smiles, wags the goopy spoon at the statue. "Yes, you make your point."

Ram scrunches up his face. This Nek is out of his mind.

"Here it is, then." Nek resumes working. "You are my favorite so far."

That's it? This statue is his favorite? His favorite what?

"I know, I know," Nek says. "But I see the differences. You're all different. You're all closer to being right than the time before."

Different? Closer?

"Perhaps I shouldn't play favorites." Nek places

another shard. "But I'm in good enough company, aren't I? Even King Dasaratha had his favorites, and we all know how that turned out."

King Dasaratha? Ram knows India has a prime minister, not a king. What is this Nek talking about?

"No?" Nek asks the statue, sounding almost annoyed. "You don't know?"

Despite himself, despite the fact that he is hiding in the tree and the tangled vines, Ram feels himself shaking his head.

"Then listen."

Long, long ago, in a corner of the land that would one day be called India, Dasaratha ruled the beautiful kingdom of Ayodhya. To help him rule, King Dasaratha had the wise and beautiful Kausalya at his side. But while the people of the kingdom lived in peace and wealth, the king and his wife were unhappy.

They had no children.

Desperate for an heir, the king took a second wife, Sumitra.

Still no sons or daughters.

So he took a third wife, Kaikeyi. Kaikeyi had saved

the king's life when they first met, and because of it he had promised to grant her two wishes someday. And Dasaratha was sure she would be the one to finally bear him a child.

Once again, the household despaired when no children were born of this union either.

Now Dasaratha had three beautiful wives—though Kausalya remained his favorite—but no children to carry on his kingdom.

One god in particular saw his despair and decided to help.

His name was Vishnu.

Vishnu sent a holy man to Dasaratha, a holy man bearing a magic bowl of *kheer*. The holy man promised the king that if he only gave his wives some of this special food, they would finally conceive and bear him sons.

Of course, the king obeyed. But because he loved Kausalya best, he gave her a portion double what he gave to the other two wives.

And lo, soon Dasaratha had not one son, but four!

To Kausalya, his most beloved wife, was born Rama.

To his middle wife, the twins Lakshmana and Shatrughna.

And to his youngest wife was born Bharata.

The entire kingdom rejoiced. Four sons! Four princes!

But Rama was special. It was obvious from the first moment all laid eyes upon him. His skin was the color of the sky on a cloudless day.

The blue cast to his skin should have been unnatural, but to all who saw the baby, it seemed the most *right* thing in the world. And the blue deepened as he grew older and even more handsome. His eyes shone with wisdom, his mind raced with understanding, and his heart beat with kindness.

He was the favorite of his father the king. Indeed the favorite of all who knew the brothers. What no one knew, not even Rama himself, was that Vishnu had entered the world through the birth of the four brothers. Because Rama's mother had taken a bigger portion of the magic *kheer*, the lion's share of Vishnu's strength and virtue rested inside Rama, ready and waiting for the time when it would be required.

King Dasaratha and Queen Kausalya were proud of their Rama, and in their hearts they knew the first prince was meant for something greater than simply inheriting his father's throne.

So when the holy man came back to Ayodhya many years later, the king and queen were not surprised to find that he had a special interest in Rama. They were, however, surprised by his request.

"Dear King Dasaratha," the holy man said. "There is a sacred place just beyond your borders where I wish to pray."

"Go freely, wise one," the king said, "and go with my blessing."

The holy man bowed his thanks, but continued, "I would go, good king, but for one problem."

In those days, many *rakshasas*, or evil creatures, walked the earth. Some only pestered the good people, but some were very dangerous and evil.

"There is a demon who devours all who seek to visit the holy place where I must go to pray."

The king, perhaps sensing what the holy man was about to ask for, made him an offer. "I will send my finest soldiers along with you to protect you and slay the demon."

The wise man shook his head. "I need only two strong warriors."

"Two?"

The holy man nodded. "Your sons, Rama and Lakshmana."

Dasaratha's heart wilted. Rama was the king's favorite, but Lakshmana was a near second. And the two brothers were also the best of friends. "But they have only just come into their manhood. Surely my trained—"

The holy man lifted a hand to silence him. "Your trained soldiers are fine for protecting your borders. But your princes have within them strong spirits."

As king, Dasaratha could have refused the holy man. But he knew his sons were special. Their births were special; their lives so far had been special. The king knew all along that their destinies could be no less important. And he knew he alone could not prepare Rama and Lakshmana for what might await them. This holy man could. "You will bring them back safely?"

"I promise. But it is I who need their protection. They need only my teaching. And I will teach them all I can." The holy man knew how much of Vishnu was hidden within Rama and Lakshmana, even though they had no notion of it themselves.

The king explained to his sons why the holy man had come.

Rama and Lakshmana's eyes flashed at each other. At last! Life in a palace in a peaceful kingdom is all very well and good for a time, but Rama and his brother were eager for adventure.

But they were also loyal sons who saw how much it pained their father to even consider letting them go. Rama stuffed down his eagerness and asked his father, "Do you wish us to go with him?"

King Dasaratha nodded gravely. "It is my wish that you learn from him and then return to me."

Rama and Lakshmana bowed low, letting the grins break on their faces for the first time.

Ram awakes, jerking his head back and knocking it hard against the tree trunk. His left leg is asleep from bracing himself into his perch. When he tries to move it, he loses his balance and tumbles sideways out of the tree.

Oof. The wind rushes from his lungs as he lands on the soft forest floor. He gasps for air, still trying to get his numb leg to move. Then he remembers the bicycle man. Nek.

He sits up, the air just starting to find its way back into his lungs. The fires have gone out. Moonlight trickles through branches overhead, and Ram can make out the profile of the stone warrior statue still in the place where the man had been working.

But then he realizes he is alone! He can search for his money in peace.

Ram scans the ground around the statue, sees nothing. That Nek fellow may be *pagal*, but he wouldn't likely leave a small fortune lying out in the open. Ram goes to the tarp sheltering the pile of junk, half limping as he stamps out the pins and needles pricking at his sleepy leg.

It is too dark under the tarp to see much. Instead he feels inside jars and boxes and bags. He finds sand. Then his hand recoils when something sharp pokes his fingers. One box clinks promisingly, but when he holds it up to the light, it is full of soda bottle caps. His heart leaps when his fist closes around a corner of soft cotton, but when he pulls it free, it is only a ragged old sari.

A sensible man would have taken the money with him. But Nek can't be sensible, not after what Ram observed, how the man told the story to the statue—

The story. The king. The princes. One of them named Rama. He must be the figure from the shrine with the blue skin. Maybe the other one, the scary-looking one—is the brother the holy man took along with Rama. Did Rama know, Ram wonders, that he was more than just a prince? How could he not? How could he not wake up every day and know his life was meant for more?

Ram knows that feeling. It sneaks up on him sometimes—the hope that he is more than just a kid who has been left behind. The quiet, stubborn faith that someone will come along and claim him or call him out for an adventure. That he might have more of a story.

It stirs in him now, that feeling. But he can't sit around waiting. He can't afford it.

Ram steps back to survey the tarp and its contents. It's too dark. He'll have to sneak back when it's light and make a proper search.

Or perhaps it isn't in the pile of junk. He eyes the stones circling the work space. Then he drops to his knees and goes to each rock, one by one, and tips it up to see if maybe his money is hidden beneath. He makes it halfway around the circle when he realizes there is another trail leading deeper into the jungle.

Ha! The *pagal* man must have a proper hut deeper within. A proper place where he'd live and where he'd have taken Ram's money. Ram springs to his feet and follows the twisting path. Suddenly a quacking, clicking sound makes him freeze. But then Ram recognizes the gecko's chirp and knows the sticky-footed lizard can't hurt him. Still, he's nervous, alone in this forest, and his hand finds the watch on his wrist. He presses the buttons with his thumb, comforted by the thin little beeping sounds.

After only a few dozen meters, Ram arrives at a wall covered in something bumpy, something rough and indiscernible in the moonlight, but the gap in it, the low arched doorway, is unmistakable.

The back of his neck tingles. He is in a strange place created by an odd man. And there are probably even now snakes eager to drop on him.

Still, he creeps closer to the door and pokes his head through, hands braced on either side against the sharp edges of whatever is stuccoed on the wall.

His knees buckle.

Hundreds of stone warriors stand arrayed on two slopes rising up from both sides of the path. Hundreds of figures nearly identical to the one Nek made tonight. They are too many, their eyes staring at him, and all the little fears expand inside him like a sail filling with fresh wind.

Ram bolts from the wall and crashes through

the forest toward the road. He doesn't stop as he passes the clearing with the banyan where he hid. He doesn't stop when his tunic snags the thorn of a low-hanging acacia. The fabric rips and the branch springs back behind him, raining its heavy dark pods onto the path. He doesn't stop when he reaches the open air and the glow of the lights from Sector 22.

He doesn't stop running until he is home.

R am doesn't know what to do with himself the
next morning.

He slept little, stewing over his lost fortune, Nek,
and the army of statues that scared him so.

But he also can't stop thinking about Rama's story.
It feels familiar. Like an echo of a voice instead of the
voice itself. He supposes if the story has to do with
the figures in the shrine or the festivals this time of
year, maybe he's absorbed some of the tale without
even knowing it. Maybe last night was just the first
time he'd heard it laid out like that from the beginning, the first time the pieces started to fit together.

But a story won't feed him. So with his stomach rumbling, his mind still whirling, he creeps out from his hidden nest and makes his way to street level. He has his portion of the money that he reclaimed from the shrine. He could buy something, but there might be another way—there often is. His hollow belly urges him to hurry. The woman who runs the dancing school is standing on the sidewalk, supervising a pair of workmen who are repainting the lettering on her windows. She gives Ram a glance, crosses her arms, and goes back to scolding the painters. Ram pulls a branch of the neem tree planted in the strip in front of her studio, peels back the bark, and chews up the end, fraying it into bristles before scrubbing at his teeth. He showed Daya how to do this once, but she gagged at the bitter taste and said Ram needed a proper toothbrush and the minty paste she used.

As Ram finishes his cleaning, Sonny the vegetable wallah pushes his cart past the samosa stand. "Go-biiiiiiii! Se-baaaaa! A-looooooo!" His voice rises at the end of each word calling out the cauliflower, apples, potatoes he has for sale today. Sometimes he'll toss a bruised banana Ram's way, but today he doesn't even meet his eye.

But Mr. Govinder Singh does. "Hey, Ram," he says, stepping out of the way of Sonny's cart and onto the sidewalk. He holds a bulging paper sack blotted with grease. Samosas from Rakesh.

Ram smiles to show off his clean teeth. Maybe Mr. Singh's bought enough to share?

"Hello, Uncle ji," he says. To others, Singh is Mr. Singh. To Daya, he is Papa. To Ram, he is simply Singh, or uncle. Ram knows how lucky he is to have a friend like Singh, and how fortunate it is to have someone of quality who looks out for him rather than down their nose at him. "What can I do for you today? Laundry picked up? Or do you have a book on order that I can—"

"Nice watch," Singh says, glaring at Ram's wrist.

Ram holds it up proudly. "Almost as nice as yours! Look at—"

"Daya told me what happened yesterday afternoon." Singh's voice is stern.

"Oh." Ram's shoulders go slack. Daya and her big mouth.

"You're taking a *panga*, keeping something like that, Ram. And I don't like you involving my daughter in your schemes." Singh is taller than anyone Ram has ever seen. He wears his hair wound up in a sky-blue *dastar*. His beard is tidy as always, the black giving way to silver slowly. His legs seem almost too long for his body and he moves deliberately, walking like he is afraid of breaking something. Ram asked him once why he moved like that, why he wasn't a soldier or policeman like so many of the other Sikhs. And Singh told him that he had been a soldier when he was younger. He'd even fought in the last war with Pakistan—the short one—and been injured somehow, though Ram couldn't get him to tell any more about it.

"It wasn't like that, Uncle ji! Those boys—"

Singh holds up a hand. "I don't care what it was like. Keep Daya out of your gambling."

"It isn't gambling if I never lose."

The ghost of a smile flits over Singh's face. He's like this, Singh. A year ago, on a day when Ram must have looked even hungrier than he felt, Singh called down from his open window on the second floor of the government building, "I'll give you two paisa if you bring me a cup of chai from the wallah in Sector Thirty-Two." Ram jumped to his feet, caught the rupee coin Singh dropped from the window, and rushed to the next sector for the tea.

Since then, it has been little jobs a few times a

week. Dropping laundry with the washerwomen. Carrying letters to the post office. Fetching deliveries to his house in 19. That was how he met Mrs. Singh—a steely-eyed woman who spoke sharply to Ram when he turned up with parcels, who *never* offered him food. It was also at the house in 19 that he first met Daya, though they didn't speak until much later. That wasn't until the day when Singh missed his train.

Singh had gone to Delhi on business that morning. But there were protests and troubles in the capital that afternoon, and Singh was unable to catch the express train back. But no one told Daya, who turned up at Singh's office after school. She waited outside the office for an hour, then another, before Ram saw her sitting there. He'd had nothing better to do, so he sat with her and kept her company. When it began to grow dark and all the other workers in the building headed home, he could tell Daya was worried that something had happened to her father.

"He's probably already home by now," Ram said. "He just forgot he was supposed to meet you."

Daya wrinkled her nose. "He doesn't forget."

"Then you'll sit here all night?" Ram asked.

Daya looked nervously at the building behind her and then into the dusky lane that led back to 19. "No."

"Take a cycle rickshaw home, or a *tuk-tuk*," Ram suggested. "I'll wait here for Singh to tell him you've gone ahead."

"I don't have any money."

Ram didn't either. "So we'll walk," he said. "I know the way."

Daya looked offended. "I know the way to my own house!"

But she let him walk her home.

Mrs. Singh had been frantic when Daya showed up at the front door, while Ram lingered under the maples that lined the front walk. But the next morning Singh had sought him out and thanked him for his help.

A few weeks after that, Daya had a holiday from school and Singh brought her to work with him. She asked to play with Ram, following him around like a moony goat. He did the only thing he knew how to do: taught her to hit *gilli*.

And since then, she seemed to find him, using some sixth sense to home in on him at any park throughout the city of Chandigarh. Daya was his audience, accomplice, and acolyte all in one. He supposed that was the closest to a friend he'd ever have.

"What is to become of you, Ram?" Singh asks, waving Ram over to the samosa stand. "Two more, Rakesh."

Ram tries for humble and contrite, but the promise of food fouls up his self-control and he does a little shuffle with his feet.

Rakesh mutters to himself, but he reaches under the clean white towel for the vegetarian samosas.

"Not those!" Ram can't help himself, waving at the pile under the red towel. "The meat ones!"

Rakesh freezes, eyes narrow. He brandishes the tongs at Ram. "You should be grateful—"

Singh shrugs him off. "He can have the lamb, Rakesh."

"*Shukriya*, Uncle ji," Ram says.

"This man is very important in Chandigarh!" Rakesh wags the tongs at Singh as he glares at Ram. "Show respect! Address him as *Sri* Singh!"

"It is all right, Rakesh," Singh says. "I told him to call me uncle."

"Thank you, Uncle ji." Ram grins.

Rakesh bites his lip, snatches two fat samosas from the other pile, and drops them roughly in a square of newspaper. He passes it to Ram and accepts the coins from Singh.

"*Shukriya*," Singh says.

Rakesh nods, dropping the money in his apron pocket and then sliding his glance at Ram to give him the stinkeye. But Ram is already halfway through the first samosa.

He follows Singh to the steps of the municipal building. Singh sits. Ram stays on his feet, keeping his distance.

"Maybe if you're fed, you'll keep out of trouble today," Singh says.

Ram's mouth is too full to make promises he won't keep.

They eat quietly for a moment.

When the edge of Ram's hunger has dulled, he slows down to savor the second samosa. "How is your work going, Uncle ji?"

Ram knows a little about what Singh does. He is a sort of engineer, in charge of planning out the roads and supervising the crews and the placement of the new buildings in the city. He is, as Rakesh said, very important.

"Fine," Singh says without enthusiasm. "The roads get built, straight and sure. The buildings do too."

"I saw workmen digging out the ground in the middle of Twenty-Six," Ram says. "What's going there?"

Singh brightens. "That will be something. Chandigarh is to have a museum! The mayor has decided if we are going to be the city everyone hopes we will be, we have to have all the things the other great cities of the world have. Like universities and museums." He pauses, tilts his chin at Ram. "You know what a museum is, don't you?"

Ram moves his head noncommittally. He has no idea.

"A place to display art. So other people can enjoy it."

"A whole building? For that? *Oye.*"

Singh is shocked. "Of course! Art is important."

To Ram, important things are those that can be eaten, or worn, or saved in order to one day have enough money to *do* something important.

"Like your bead," he says now to Ram. "That's art. Someone made that. Maybe for you. Or maybe just picked for you."

Ram's never thought of it as anything but the link from him to the girl. He told Singh about her last year when he first saw Ram's bead. When Ram told him how he came by it, about the girl he was beginning to forget, Singh asked many questions. Then he grew quiet and sad. Finally he sent Ram off with twenty whole rupees to buy him a copy of the Sikh newspaper, which cost only twenty-five paisa. When Ram got back, Singh was already gone.

He never asked for the paper or his change.

Singh wipes his fingers on his trousers. "Did you know that I used to love to draw? When I was your age?"

It is impossible for Ram to imagine Singh at his age.

"I thought I might grow up to be an artist," Singh confesses. "But even if I'd been good enough, my father wouldn't have allowed it. You can't make much of a living as an artist. Even all the famous painters of Europe were poor during their lives. The paintings only became valuable long after they died. So I studied engineering. Building. Architecture. At least I still get to draw some—"

"Govinder!" A round-bellied man emerges from the building. "Your assistant said you might be here!"

Singh pushes to his feet. "My morning break, commissioner. What can I do for you?"

The commissioner has eyebrows like the crests of

the hoopoe birds that forage on the play fields at the park. Red and black, feathered at the ends and flipping upward. The man is a head shorter than Singh at least, but the way Ram's friend drops his eyes and widens his stance erases the difference.

When the commissioner spins on his heel and points up the street, Singh gives Ram a quick nod to tell him he'll see him later and then follows his boss.

The morning is shaping up well enough, Ram decides. His belly is not so empty as it was an hour ago. And the sun is bright enough for searching.

It's time to go back and claim his money.

He skips around the corner, walking up the block past the gates of the factory. The man's bicycle with the crate mounted to the back is there again. Good.

Ram lingers perhaps longer than he should, because the guard comes out of the little gatehouse, hands on his hips.

"What do you want?"

Ram doesn't answer. He has what he needs. The thief Nek is working. Now Ram can go and find his money.

9

The forest is different in the daylight. A grand rosewood tree shadows the spot where the path begins, its crooked trunk and red grooved bark curving over the path. The leaves tremble in the breeze, the *shush-shush* sound like a warning. Still, Ram walks more boldly this time with the sun slipping through the gaps in the canopy overhead. His steps startle a long-eared hare that springs into the scrub and disappears.

He reaches the makeshift workshop inside the clearing quickly and is relieved to see the statue hasn't moved. Feeling braver by the moment, he creeps nearer to look at it properly. Its eyes are large and round and white, with dark pebbles set at their centers for pupils. The head—covered in a sort of helmet made of broken shards—balances atop a curved neck. Bottle caps form a studded belt at the waist, and Ram can imagine a sword hanging there.

It is just like the others on the hillside. Ram shivers under the statue's glare. The sooner he gets out of here, the better.

He searches in the bowls of cracked washbasins, avoids the lid of a Western-style toilet, and rummages through an entire crate full of light-socket receptacles.

No money.

He picks through bundles of old rags and cloth, moves cans of paint stacked like a child's blocks, sides marked in dry cascades of scarlet, orange, black, green.

No money.

The barrel of what he thought were sticks the night before is actually an assortment of reinforcing steel rods of various lengths, ends mangled and oddly bent.

But no money.

He opens countless paper bags to find them half-full of mortar and concrete mix.

Still no money.

He checks a box of bangles, finds they are all worthless: broken, bent, and mashed together so that they can never be worn again.

And his money isn't hiding here either.

He dives deeper under the tarp, growing more frustrated and careless as he shoves things around, raising so great a racket that he can't hear Nek approaching.

"Hey!"

Ram freezes. He is hemmed inside the tarp. The junk is piled up so high on the sides and at the back that the only way out is through the front where the man stands.

"What are you doing here?" Nek seems taller up close. A little younger than Ram realized at first.

Ram fakes left but then dashes right, a move he's used a hundred times before when playing tag. But the man who is not so old is also not so slow. His hand closes around Ram's forearm and yanks him back. "Not so fast!"

Ram tries to shake loose, but the man's grip is strong. "You stole my money!" Ram shouts.

Nek's features, sharpened by shock and anger, soften in confusion. "What?"

"My money!" Ram takes another half a step forward and another half a step sideways. "It landed by your bicycle and then you put some of it at the shrine, but I want it back. All of it."

"Your . . ." Understanding breaks like a sunrise. "And I thought the goddess had seen fit to bless with me with a windfall. . . ."

Emboldened by the fact that Nek has not tried to cuff him or shoo him away, Ram holds out a filthy hand. "Give it back."

Nek lowers a gleaming metal tiffin box to the dirt. "I don't have it."

"Yes, you do! I saw you with it! I saw you bring it here last night. Give it over!"

Nek digs into his pocket and pulls out Ram's bundle. "I don't have it," he says, breaking the knot and unfolding the cloth, "because I've already spent it."

Ram can only stare. There is nothing there but the crumbs from the roti and his best *gilli* stick.

The money is gone. All of it.

It would have lasted Ram a month. This fool Nek has squandered it in a day?

"Get it back!" Ram demands.

"I bought a third-class train ticket. I could not return it even if I wanted to."

A train ticket! Ram is furious and jealous all at once. Why hadn't he ever bought a train ticket? He never dreamed he had enough money for such a treasure.

Ram's fury builds. He glares at the stupid statue with its stupid eyes and thinks about all its stupid brothers arrayed on the slope deeper in the jungle. And he remembers something Singh said . . . something about art, how valuable it is. If people are foolish enough to buy paintings, surely this statue has to be worth something.

"Then give me one of your statues!" Ram snaps his finger. "I'll sell it and we'll be even."

The force of Nek's answer is stunning. "Impossible!"

"You have dozens!" Ram shouts back. "I've seen them—"

"You've seen them." Nek's storm drops to a whisper. And Ram realizes that he has spooked the man somehow.

"You have plenty to spare. One should do it—"

Nek holds up a hand. "No!" He pinches the *gilli*

stick from the cloth and holds it up. "I'll play you for it."

Ram's mouth hangs open in shock. Play him for it? He's impressed that the man even knows what the stick is for, but he guesses he was a boy once too. Maybe he played *gilli* with friends—the way it was meant to be done—scoring runs while the *gilli* is in play. But that's not what Nek is proposing now.

Nek speaks quickly. "If I beat you, you leave my statues alone. And you go away."

"But what about when I beat you?"

"You won't," Nek says simply.

Now Ram almost doesn't even care what the stakes are. He just wants to beat this man like he beats all those kids in the park. "I will. And then you'll have to give me *two* of the statues to sell."

Nek makes a face. "They're probably not worth anything, anyway."

Ram is unconvinced. Trying to make something seem worthless is the surest way to keep someone from stealing it, he guesses. He crosses his arms.

Nek shrugs. "Fine." he says. "One hit each. Farthest hit wins."

Ram snatches the stick from Nek's hand. "Fine."

He's a little worried that he might lose his lucky *gilli* in this undergrowth. But he didn't hit with it last time and that turned out terribly. He needs the luck it brings, so he'll spend hours looking for it later if he must.

Just outside the clearing, he finds a stout branch the length of his forearm. He peels a scrap of bark that clings to it like an old scab. It will serve fine as the *danda* to bat with. He doesn't need anything special to teach this goat-eyed thief a lesson.

"You want to pick your own bat?"

Nek waves him off. "Just hit."

Ram is wondering how much he can get for one of the statues. Maybe Singh will buy it.

Ram places the *gilli* on the ground at the far end of the clearing. He lines up the shot, eyeing the path leading back to the road. He glances up at Nek.

"Get on with it," Nek says.

Ram taps the end of the branch gently on the ground just in front of the *gilli* stick. Then he quickly lifts and lowers the bat so it strikes down on the front end of the *gilli*, sending it spinning up into the air. As it climbs and reaches Ram's hips, he cocks back, swings parallel to the ground, and smacks the *gilli*, sending it sailing. It flies the few meters over the clearing and lands in the trodden path beyond.

Ram paces off the distance. Certainly not his best, but it should be plenty far. He places a stone on the spot the *gilli* fell and trots back over to Nek to surrender the tools.

"One hit," Ram reminds him, eager to get this over with.

Nek does not respond. He lines up the *gilli* where Ram started. He doesn't hesitate—doesn't even take a warm-up swing—before he brings the branch down, flips up the *gilli*, and then swings sidearmed, connecting with a satisfying crack of wood on wood.

Ram is dumbstruck as the *gilli* soars over the rock he placed as a marker.

Oye.

Nek collects the *gilli* and hands it back to Ram. "Go," Nek says simply. Not unkindly, just without surprise or ceremony. Ram still can't believe what has happened.

"But . . . how?" Ram manages.

"I didn't have many friends when I was your age either," Nek says. "I taught myself to hit."

His money. All of it! Gone! How could he have lost?

There has to be something he can do. "Two out of three?" Ram tries not to sound desperate.

Nek's gaze is as steady as that of his soldiers. "A bargain is a bargain."

"But that was all my money," Ram says, still disbelieving.

Nek softens a little. "I'd give it back if I had it to give."

Ram can't leave empty-handed. "You really have nothing?"

Nek shakes his head. "That ticket was dear. I won't have money again until Saturday. Now, go, I have work to do. Something you should consider instead of gambling. Work may be slower, but there is honor in it."

Ram looks around. He's not opposed to work. He works for Singh when he can. But there aren't many jobs for boys like him. Unless . . .

"Your work here? Or work at the factory?"

"Both. And double now, thanks to the mess you've made." Nek kicks at a rat's nest of electrical wire.

"Then let me help," Ram says. "I can do jobs for you. You can pay me back a little at a time—"

"I have very little to spare."

Nek hasn't said no. Ram takes a step forward. "A

few paisa a week. I'll tidy up, or"—he gestures at the statue, searching for the words—"or whatever you need me to do to help with those."

"I don't need your help."

"You just said I should work instead of gamble. Didn't you mean it?"

"I didn't mean work for me!" But the man is thinking it over, Ram can tell. Just like when someone is considering taking a wager with him in the park. They maybe know they shouldn't, but they can't help themselves all the same. "It would take weeks to earn it back."

He still hasn't said no.

"I am a good worker."

Nek scratches the stubble at his neck. "On one condition."

"Name it."

"Tell no one about this place. Or me."

"Why not?"

Nek's eyes flash. "Do you want the job or not?"

"Yes, Uncle ji," Ram says. "And I won't tell. I have no one to tell anyway."

Nek lifts a shoulder, but he is wary. Still, a deal is a deal, Ram decides. It isn't what he came for, but at least it isn't nothing.

"I suppose you'll want to be fed, too." Nek sinks to his knees and opens the tiffin.

Ram hadn't dared to hope, but wouldn't dream of refusing.

Nek portions out a few spoonfuls of cooked rice and chickpea curry into the lid of the tiffin. "I should warn you that I am a terrible cook."

Ram takes it. "Thank you, Sri Nek."

Panic animates Nek's face. "How do you know my name?"

"Yesterday. The man at the factory called you that. And last night when you were talking to the statue, you called yourself that."

His eyes narrow. "You *were* here."

Ram squats down to eat. "My name is Ram."

Nek tilts his head to one side. "Figures."

"There was a prince named Rama in your story," Ram says. "He was the favorite, wasn't he?"

Nek doesn't answer.

"What happened to them next?"

Nek stops, a pinch of rice and curry frozen halfway to his mouth. "No one ever told you about Rama and Lakshmana?"

Ram feels a pang of shame. Why doesn't he know these stories? It seems all of India does except himself. Daya knows about them, he is sure, though he's been too embarrassed to ask her. Maybe they teach the stories in school. Or maybe her parents told them to her. He imagines the girl used to tell them to him. Maybe that's why they seem familiar?

He considers lying, acting like he's heard the stories so Nek won't think he's ignorant. But to his surprise, he realizes he wants to know the rest of the story more than he wants his pride. So he shakes his head no.

Nek looks at Ram with an expression so sad that Ram has to look away.

"What?" Ram says finally. "They're just stories."

Nek's voice is quiet. "Stories are never just stories. Especially not this one. Rama's story is the story of all of India. It is the story of good triumphing over evil. It is every story ever told wrapped into one. It is a million stories and a single story all at once. It has woven itself into every part of India. Our faith. Our history. Our holidays. Our culture. Our art."

Ram doesn't quite follow what Nek means, but he wants to. "Is that why we have parades about it? The holidays?"

"Yes," Nek says. "Dussehra first, with the pageants and the parades and the giant statues and the bonfires."

"Dussehra is now and Diwali is later," Ram says with confidence. He does know this much at least, even if no one has ever taken the time to explain it to him. He knows that soon enough people will clean up and set out lights and colorful *rangoli* will appear in the doorways—dyed grains and pulses arranged in intricate patterns. But if the stories are as much a part of India as Nek says they are, maybe they are part of Ram, too? "But what do Dussehra and Diwali have to do with the story?"

"Dussehra celebrates an important moment from the middle of the story, Diwali the ending."

"Are there parties for the beginning, too?"

"No," Nek says simply. "Endings are always more important."

Ram scratches the back of his neck. "But why? Why all this for a story? Do people believe it really happened?"

A breeze skitters along the treetops. The banyan's upper branches squeak against one another. Nek twists to look up at the spot the sound comes from. It is a long time before he speaks again. "Every religion—Hinduism included—tells stories. The Muslims have stories. The Christians. The Buddhists. I like many of their stories, too."

"But you don't believe in it? In Rama's, I mean?"

Nek looks offended. "Of course I do. But that isn't the point. The point is that stories are the way we see the truth. Even the made-up ones. Sometimes especially the made-up ones."

"So which one is it?" Ram asks, growing frustrated. "Real or made up?"

"Both," Nek says.

Ram looks at the Lakshmana statue. How many times has this story been right in front of him and he hasn't known what he was looking at? And he realizes that no matter which parts are real and which are not, he wants to hear it all.

"So will you tell me, Uncle ji?"

"Why should I?" Nek sounds annoyed. "Our bargain didn't include me telling you the *Ramayana*."

"You said yourself everybody should know it. If you believe that, you'll tell me."

Ram glimpses what he thinks might be a smile as Nek sips from a dented canteen. "I suppose you won't leave me alone unless I do. Where did I leave off? Ah, so the king's wives ate some magic *kheer* and then four princes—"

"No, no," Ram says around a mouthful of food. "You already did that part. The holy man had already come to take Rama and the other one"—he points at the statue Nek had been working on last night—"on an adventure."

"Already that far along?" Nek tilts his head sideways.

"Uh-huh."

"Oh. Don't interrupt me again."

Ram wouldn't dare.

10

The holy man, Rama, and Lakshmana walked for many days. As they traveled, Lakshmana and Rama hunted game and gathered fruit for their meals. When they rested, the holy man taught them special prayers and verses from the scriptures that increased their strength and courage. Soon the adventure and the holy man's instruction had molded two strong princes into powerful warriors.

One evening they camped beneath a stately banyan tree in the middle of a clearing. The green canopy spanned wide and perfectly round. The tree's many trunks roped together, like the pillars of a great temple.

"You know about the banyan trees, yes?" the holy man asked.

Rama answered, "I know that they are sacred. I know that the roots grow up and down the tree, connecting heaven, earth, and the underworld."

"The spirits can travel those roots," the holy man said, "passing between the realms. But this tree is many times the size that it was when last I came here to pray."

"Why?" Lakshmana asked.

The holy man placed a hand on one of the twisting roots. "This is the place I told you about. Many, many souls have died here. Tomorrow you will face the demon. It is said that this demon is impossible to kill, but at the least, try to protect me as I say the prayers at sunrise."

Lakshmana sprang to his feet. "Why wait! Rama and I can slay the demon now!"

"The demon cannot live in so holy a place. She fears the tree and spirits and the darkness. But when

I begin my prayers, she will fly here to devour me."

Rama laid a hand on the hilt of his dagger. "Lakshmana and I will be ready, guru. We will remember all you have taught us."

The next morning, when the horizon began to glow pink, the holy man knelt beneath the tree and began to pray.

His words rose up like music, joining the gentle chorus of the jungle's waking sounds. The princes found the steady rhythm of the prayer pulling them into the holy man's trance.

"Careful, brother," Rama warned. "Stand ready."

Then a great thrashing shook the trees in the forest beyond, and a moaning howl drowned out the sound of the prayers. In a moment, a giant demon—red eyes rolling in deep sockets, snaggly teeth bared—charged into the clearing. The holy man did not move or even open his eyes. The demon leveled its twisting horns and charged at the holy man, not seeing Rama and Lakshmana standing by.

Lakshmana drew his saber; Rama nocked an

arrow in his bow and let it fly. The demon's cry pitched higher as the arrow found its mark in the left eye. It then saw Rama standing there, and it bellowed even louder in rage. It charged Rama, tugging the arrow from its eye and casting it aside. Rama readied another arrow, pulled back his bowstring, and took a steadying breath.

But he never had to loose the arrow. Suddenly the demon faltered, threw back its head, and stared at the sky. Once again the sound of the holy man's words filled the clearing.

Then, with a great crash like a falling tree, the demon toppled. As it fell, Lakshmana stood atop the monster's back, wiping clean his sword.

Rama and Lakshmana clasped each other's forearms and gave thanks for their victory. Then the demon's body began to smolder. Fire seemed to grow from within the body of the beast itself. Rama and Lakshmana gaped as scale and horn and claw and fang burned into a tiny pile of white ash.

They were still staring when the holy man finished his prayers and rose. He scattered the ash with his dusty foot and then strode across the clearing. "Come."

"But, teacher," Rama said, "home is that way."

The holy man walked on. "There are many ways to reach home," he said. "And there is yet more for you to see and learn before we return."

11

"Where did they go?"

"Another time." Nek stands. "My lunch break is over soon."

Ram is surprised to see that he has licked clean his own dish. He doesn't remember eating a single bite—only the story. He thinks of how easily Rama and Lakshmana handled the demon. If only he had as simple a time with that bunch of *bewakoofs* who had chased him and started all this trouble.

Ram hands the dish back to Nek. "I'll stay here and clean up the junk—"

"No!"

"But—"

"I said no! You are not to be here without me!" Nek's voice is firm. "You do it tonight. When I finish at the factory."

"But it is only tidying—"

"And no sleeping here."

"I have a good place to sleep," Ram says, thinking he doesn't really need to confess that he already fell asleep here once. Though with the weather turning, he'll need to start collecting cardboard and hauling it up to the rooftop to fill in the gaps in his sleeping berth, or maybe even find a different place to sleep out the colder months altogether. *It would be nice to have a place to stay all year,* he thinks, *with windows to catch the breeze in summer and to shut tight in winter.*

But Rama didn't need a palace. Ram doesn't need windows.

"*Chalo.*" At the street, Nek climbs onto his bicycle. "You may work this evening. After you've had your supper. I can't feed you again today."

He pedals off, but Ram is quick enough to keep pace with the bike. "You come every day? During lunch and after you work at the factory?"

"Most days," Nek says.

"Then I can earn my money back quickly," Ram says.

Nek snorts. "You can earn it back when I can afford to pay you."

They reach the heart of the sector. Nek dismounts the bike and pushes it the rest of the way to the gate. In the distance, Ram can hear the loudspeaker mounted to the wall outside the Sikh temple blaring the droning prayers, the harmonium buzzing along with it. "Bye," Ram says. Nek ignores him as he joins the other workers reentering the factory gates.

"Ram!" Singh is standing at the end of the lane. He waves Ram over. Ram rushes to him and finds Daya with fists clenched, feet planted, wearing a scowl as severe as the part in her hair.

"Hello, Uncle ji!" Ram says.

Singh points at the factory gates. "Who was that man you were walking with?"

Ram shrugs. "No one." He turns to Daya. "Shouldn't you be in school?"

Daya pulls a face, but Singh speaks before she can. "She should. But she came looking for you. And now you are going to make sure she gets back to school before she misses any more of her lessons—"

"I don't need him to nanny me!" Daya stoops slightly with the weight of the books in her knapsack. Does one of them have the story of Rama inside it? Maybe school wouldn't be so terrible if some of those books had things like that to read. But Daya complains enough about grammar and penmanship to lessen the temptation.

"Maybe not. But if the one person you're out searching for actually escorts you to school, then at least I know you'll be delivered," Singh says firmly. His tone grows even gruffer when he speaks to Ram. "Hire a *tuk-tuk*. You won't make it in time otherwise."

A *tuk-tuk*! Ram tries to hide his joy. He's only ridden one once before.

"And my fee?" Ram asks, snatching a pair of ten-rupee notes from Singh's hand.

Singh rolls his eyes. "There's plenty there for the fare and your fee. Just go!"

"*His* fee!" Daya squeaks. "When he owes *me* for—"

Ram grabs her hand and begins dragging her to the corner where the auto rickshaws wait. "Sure thing!"

Singh gives his daughter another stern glance.

"We'll speak about this again at home," he says, adding, "With your mother."

Daya's eyes grow big as onions. "She doesn't have to know, does she, Papa?"

Ram smirks. He knows enough about Mrs. Singh to understand why Daya is afraid.

Singh considers, but doesn't answer. "Go to school. I'll see you at home."

Ram can't believe his luck. Since yesterday's calamity, he's been fed twice, secured a job, and now gets to go for a fast ride in an auto rickshaw.

Daya drags her feet as Ram pulls her toward the *tuk-tuk* stand. "You're so lucky you don't have to go to school."

"Won't you be out for the holiday soon?"

"Not till Saturday." Daya flips her braids. "It isn't fair. All the older kids don't even come this week. I don't see why I—"

"Because you're not older," Ram says, holding tightly to Daya's wrist.

Daya is probably only a couple of years younger than Ram, but he has no way to be sure, since he isn't sure how old *he* actually is. Judging from the size of other kids, and how he hasn't lost any baby teeth for over a year, he and Daya worked out that he must be at least twelve, maybe as old as thirteen. Daya is only ten.

All the *tuk-tuk* drivers ignore them at first, feet up on the front seats as they lounge in the back, chatting and smoking. Then Ram holds up the money, and the one nearest them tosses his cigarette to the ground. "Where do you girls want to go?"

Daya snickers into her hand. Ram fumes. His hair is too long, he knows. But still, how can anyone think he's a *girl*? He forces his voice lower. "Bhavan Vidyalya in Thirty-Three!"

Their driver does a double take; the others hoot and whistle.

Ram's cheeks burn as he negotiates the fare. At least he gets a decent rate. The driver pulls the starter cord, and the engine coughs black smoke as it awakes. Ram and Daya climb in the back. Daya reaches over to tug at Ram's curls. "You should cut it, Ram."

He wishes he could. But haircuts cost money. There's a barber with a chair set up beneath a big almond tree near the lake who Ram can sometimes get to cut his hair if no one else is around. But there are usually lots of people around. Boys watched by crossed-arm mothers, making sure they get their trims. Ram can never understand why those boys are so sullen about it. He'd love to have someone to make sure his hair was tidy, and to pay the barber full price instead of whatever Ram can afford.

He swats Daya's hand away to study the driver's movements, mentally ticking off each step before the driver makes it. The driver uses his heel to drop the choke back into position, removes the parking brake, and puts both hands on the handlebar. He cranks hard to the right, twists back on the throttle, and eases the auto rickshaw toward the road. The driver thumbs the horn, laying heavy on the button. All the other cars and trucks and *tuk-tuks* on the road blare back in response. Daya holds her hands over her ears and grimaces, but Ram only smiles wider.

The *tuk-tuk* merges with the stream of vehicles and picks up speed.

Wind swirls inside the open frame. On hot days, Ram sometimes wishes for a ride just to cool him off. But today Daya wraps up tightly in her jacket, loops her scarf around her neck, and tucks her hands into her armpits.

Ram doesn't care about the cold. He grips the bar

between the driver's seat and their bench with both hands, leans his head sideways, and lets the wind lash his face. Someday he'll move this fast everywhere he goes. Someday he won't be limited by how far he can run or walk.

They beeline up the road, straight as an arrow, barely slowing as they reach the traffic circle at the corner where four sectors meet. The driver goes three-quarters of the way around, veers north, and takes that lane—as straight and wide as the last one—for almost a whole kilometer. Traffic zips by in both directions, on either side of the little median filled with scrubby grass. Alongside the street, shops and apartments and office buildings rise up, all with the same sharp right angles, the same square shapes, the terraces fronting the street sometimes bearing a clothesline or a potted lemon tree. The walkers on the sidewalk flow like a countercurrent to the traffic, the streams muddying and eddying where the pedestrians cross at the corners.

They pass the open pit where the new museum will go. The footers have been dug. A few dozen men are already dumping concrete from wheelbarrows into what will be the foundation.

At the next sector, Ram looks away as they pass the orphanage. Singh convinced Ram to try it out once. Told him about how Chandigarh was special for having one with a school attached. Ram lasted one night. He ate better on the streets, slept better on his own, and didn't have to trouble with school. Maybe the children's home was fine for babies. But he didn't belong there.

All too soon, the driver throttles back, slows, and slides off the road in front of the tall wooden gates of Daya's school. Ram hands the notes over to the driver, who hands back a smaller coin.

"*Nahi!*" Daya glares at the driver. "That wasn't the price!"

Daya does have her uses. The driver digs deeper into his pocket, pulls out another coin to match the one he's already handed to Ram. The children clamber out and the *tuk-tuk* drives away.

Daya holds out her hand. "Give it."

"What?"

"You owe me for yesterday," she insists. "Give it."

Ram groans. "I lost that money we won, Daya. All of it. Hitting."

"Someone actually beat you? Who?"

Ram wants to tell her. But he promised Nek he

wouldn't tell about the clearing in the forest. "Just some man."

"The one Papa and I saw you with? Why did you challenge him?"

"He challenged *me*," Ram says. The loss still stings.

She shakes her head. "Well, it isn't my fault you got greedy." She holds out her hand, wiggles her fingers.

Ram sighs, utters a mild curse Rakesh throws at him sometimes, and gives Daya one of the precious coins. The bell inside the school clangs, echoing to the street.

"See you after school," Daya says, starting for the front door.

"I can't," Ram says. "I have somewhere to be."

Daya stops. "Can I come?"

"You heard your father. Your *maa* wants to talk to you after school."

Ram can't resist needling her, not after she was so ruthless about the money. But she only wrinkles up her nose at him and heads inside with the other kids coming back late from lunches at home.

As Daya passes through the school gates, he hears a familiar voice call out, "Little girl!"

Ram goes still.

Peach Fuzz is just on the other side of the wall.

"Where's your *friend*?" Peach Fuzz asks.

Daya's voice comes back a little thinner than Ram is used to hearing it. "I'm going to class, Vijay."

"Your beggar pal got away last night, but we'll find him. He can't keep my watch."

"You lost it fair and square. It isn't his fault—"

"He cheated and you know it!"

Cheated! Ram is tempted to charge around the wall and tackle the boy now, though he knows it wouldn't help. And he'd be the one to get in trouble: a street kid attacking a student at his own school. And he'd surely lose the watch in the process. Besides, Daya can handle this, can't she?

"He didn't cheat! You can't even cheat at *gilli*! And you'll never find him. So leave me alone!"

Ram grins. He can picture her, toe to toe with the bully. She's safe enough. Even that bully wouldn't hurt a girl, especially one so much younger.

Then he hears the sound of something falling to the ground. "Hey!" Daya says. "Pick those up!"

"Pick up your own books. And get the watch back from that street rat. It'll go better for him if you give it to us rather than us finding him ourselves."

Daya mumbles a phrase that Ram *knows* her mother would not be pleased to hear, but another voice shouts over them. "You lot," a teacher calls. "Get to your lessons!"

Ram waits a second longer, after he hears the pack move off. Then he peeks around the gate in time to see the door swinging shut behind Daya.

He hadn't thought the watch would cause trouble for Daya, too. But after the way Peach Fuzz just treated her, he certainly doesn't deserve to get it back. And Daya's tough. She can handle it. And school will be out soon and she won't have to see them for a couple of weeks and they'll forget about it.

Won't they?

The question lingers all the long walk back to his sector.

That evening Ram helps Nek organize the supplies under the tarp. When they finish, Nek studies the statue in the middle of the ring. "I suppose it is time for him to join the others." He lights a torch from one of the burning tires and hands it to Ram. Then he hefts the statue, more easily than Ram would have guessed the man could. Hauling all those rocks has made him stronger than he appears. "*Chalo*, Ram."

Ram follows him down the path he mistakenly took last night. The path twists and bends madly, and Ram realizes why it scared him so last night: it is the exact opposite of the streets he knows so well. He wonders if Nek built it this way on purpose.

Overhead, monkeys whistle warnings and scatter as Nek and Ram wade beneath the vines and branches. Farther in, an animal plated in gray scales over his rounded back and down his long, thick tail shuffles away from a rotten log. Ram barely has time to note the pointed snout and black eyes before the creature disappears, leaving behind it a musky odor like Ram's alley on a hot summer day.

"What was that?"

"Pangolin," Nek says. "Very rare."

"Is it dangerous?"

"Only if you're an ant. But he's strong. He can roll up into a ball and not even a tiger can break through his armor. When I was your age, I startled one and it sprayed me. I stank for weeks." Ram backs away.

Soon they reach the wall studded with those odd spiky pieces.

Ram lifts a hand to test their rough edges. "What are these?"

Nek wiggles a loose one. "For holding bulbs in light fixtures. Porcelain. The collars are fragile. When they began building Chandigarh, they leveled many old villages. Some of the great mountains of trash you see around the city still are from those huts and buildings. I pulled these from those piles."

"Why didn't they just build around the villages?"

"People like new things. Fresh starts. Sometimes chucking old, worn-out things makes people hopeful." He sounds unconvinced.

"Do you wish they hadn't wrecked the villages?"

Nek takes a long time to answer. "I wish for many things. But if they hadn't torn down the villages, if they hadn't built a new city from scratch, I guess I wouldn't have supplies."

They duck under the curved doorway. Then Nek climbs up a waist-high embankment reinforced with a sloppy concrete retaining wall, and walks among the statues, a giant amid children. He waves Ram forward.

"Why do you make all of this stuff?" Ram asks.

Nek doesn't hesitate. "Because we are all created to make things. Some people make bread. Some people make clothing. Some make music—"

"And you make bicycles at the factory," Ram interrupts.

"And *you* make trouble," Nek says.

Ram looks around at the statues. "But why do you make so many of the *same* thing?"

"Why do you ask so many questions?" Nek shoots back, but Ram can tell he doesn't mean it. Nek kicks some leaves off the base of one statue. "They're not the same. They're an army. Every man in the army is a man unto himself, though when they stand together, they stand as one."

"But . . ." Ram is still not sure how *pagal* the man might be. "They're *smiling*." He recalls the soldiers he's seen marching outside the cantonment, or guarding buildings. Are they even allowed to smile?

"No." Nek carries the statue up the slope to an open space. "They're laughing."

"Laughing?"

"Have you ever laughed so hard you couldn't do anything else? Even if you tried?" Nek positions the statue on its feet. "Or have you heard another's laugh so pure that you can't help but join in?"

Ram waits. He isn't sure about either.

Nek fusses with the statue, turning it a centimeter at a time to get the angle right. "If they're laughing, they can't fight. If they're laughing, who will want to fight them?"

Ram has no idea what the man is talking about.

"No more war," Nek says, as if the answer is as

simple as the sums Daya does to make change with the rickshaw wallah.

"That's it?" Ram asks. "That's why you made all these? To stop . . . *war*?"

"Truly, boy, if you have so many questions, go to school or read a book. Don't bother me with them."

When Ram doesn't answer, Nek sighs. "You know about Partition, yes?"

Ram draws himself up taller. "My friend Singh uncle told me. And I've heard old men—older than you—talking about it. If you were Muslim, you went to live in Pakistan. If you weren't, you came to India. Bad things happened when people moved back and forth. People got killed or separated from their families."

Nek climbs back down and takes the torch from Ram.

"Why, though?" Ram persists. "Why do you make them, really?"

Nek rises. "Maybe it is easier if I just show you so you'll stop pestering me. *Chalo.*"

Ram hurries to keep up, following Nek through another arched doorway and then up a little rise.

"How big is this place?" Ram is now wondering why a man rich enough to have so much land is so stingy in paying him back.

"My garden is always growing," Nek says.

Garden? Ram starts to ask why a garden when Nek's torchlight reflects brilliantly off cobalt-blue glass. An eye. An eye in a stone tiger, its stripes made of black rubber, the bicycle tread still visible in patches. "*Wah ji wah*," Ram says. He squints into the darkness. There's a monkey. A peacock with a fanned tail made of broken dishes and mirrors. A whole menagerie. "These are—"

"Not now," Nek says.

They begin to descend again, leaving the animals behind. Finally Nek stops in front of a blob of concrete covered in vines. "I've been neglecting this corner."

Ram takes a closer look. Houses. Houses! Six, seven, maybe more. Each is big enough for a little dog to climb inside, or maybe one of the monkeys that hangs from the treetops. Their walls are made of the same rough concrete, their crude doorways stand open, their roofs are made of mismatched planks. Some are bigger than others, some taller, narrower. A couple have rounded walls, more huts than houses.

"It started here."

"A village," Ram says.

"My village." Nek brushes some dried leaves from the doorway of the nearest structure.

"One of the ones that was knocked down?"

"No," he says. "The one I left in the north. I walked here with my mother and father. Hundreds of miles we walked."

"You were one of the ones who left," Ram says, starting to understand. "How old were you?"

Nek considers. "I was only a boy. Nearly thirty years gone. My younger sister was lost."

"Lost?"

"Taken. Long before we even reached the new border. We searched for her. But she was just one person. And everybody lost someone. We had to keep going or we'd have been killed too."

"You stopped here? In Chandigarh?" Ram rubs the bead under his shirt.

Nek breathes deeply. "Delhi." He wanders over to another of the buildings. "Family there took us in until we could rent rooms of our own. My mother took in washing and my father worked as a porter. I was able to go to school for a while."

"Only for a while?"

"My father died two years after we settled. And my mother a few months after him. The breaking of

95

the country, the move . . . Damini's disappearance. Partition killed so many people. It just took longer for my parents. Like a cancer."

Ram says nothing.

"I was sent to live with other relatives. I made a life there as best I could. But work was scarce. Three years ago I came to Chandigarh to work in the bicycle factory. I found the trees one day when the factory was shut. I did not want to go back to my room on Mani Marg, so I wandered out here. And found this place." He gazes at the trees and the darkness pressing around them. "It made me remember being a boy. Playing in the forest near my old village. Plowing fields and planting crops and carrying water from the well for my father's farm. Something in me woke up. My hands wanted to make things. I saw all the extra material left over from constructing the government buildings and apartments and roads. I collected bits that they were going to throw away. And I didn't know I was rebuilding the village I left behind until I was halfway through it."

Nek lays his palm on the roof of one house.

"This is like the one I grew up in," he explains. "And that one, with the wavy roof? That was the temple."

"So you did all this—even the soldiers and the walls and everything—because you were . . . homesick?"

"At first. Now I'm so used to making things that I can't stop. I don't want to. Even though it could all be taken from me just as swiftly as my first life was."

Ram goes still. "Taken from you, Uncle ji?"

Nek stares at him, daring him to figure out what he's just said.

And Ram understands with a jolt that Nek is not supposed to be here. Just as Ram is not supposed to live on the rooftop of the dancing school, Nek has no rightful claim to this land. No wonder he uses garbage to make his statues. No wonder he works all day in a factory. No wonder he was so panicked when Ram first appeared. No wonder he made Ram promise not to tell anyone about it.

"You don't own this land. You don't belong here."

Nek climbs around to another hut to clear its door and windows. "I do belong here."

"But you don't own it. They could make you leave." Nek continues tearing at the creepers. Ram's brain is still parsing out what this all means and he speaks without thinking, blurting out, "I could just make you pay me now to keep quiet about this place." Ram is ashamed the instant the words leave his mouth. He hadn't meant it as a threat, but he knows it sounds that way.

Ram backpedals. "I didn't mean . . . I mean that I was just . . ." What does Ram mean? He means that he is glad that in some way, some *tiny* way, Nek needs or wants Ram's help. Or that he wants to share this place and this work with him. But he isn't sure how to say this without sticking his foot in his mouth again. Luckily, he doesn't have to.

"I know you won't tell. Now come and help me."

Ram is relieved that Nek knows him well enough already to know that he can keep a secret. Especially one so wonderful as this. He isn't used to being trusted. And he likes the feeling. He joins Nek to tug at the vines. "How do you know I won't say anything, Uncle ji?"

Nek waits until they pull the last of the vines free. He starts walking back up the path to the clearing, torch in hand, before he answers. "Because if you did, you would not know what happens next to Rama and Lakshmana."

13

Rama and Lakshmana were pleased to continue their adventures and their training. The holy man was pleased to have the protection and companionship the brothers offered. But he had a higher purpose in leading them farther from home.

The neighboring kingdom was ruled by wise King Janak. King Janak had a special daughter of his own. He, too, had been childless, until one day he prayed to the gods. The next morning one of his farmers plowed a field outside the palace walls. When the farmer surveyed the furrow he'd just dug, he was shocked to find a beautiful, healthy infant girl among the roots and stones. He hurried the baby to the palace. Janak recognized the girl as the answer to his pleas, adopted her, and named her Sita.

Sita grew in loveliness and kindness, and she brought joy to Janak's household. The holy man could not resist playing matchmaker. So it was he led Rama to Janak's palace. And so it was he made sure that Rama glimpsed Sita through the carved lattices on the terrace of the palace.

Both were lovestruck. Sita could scarcely credit that such perfection walked the earth. Rama could not believe he'd gone his whole life without witnessing such beauty.

Though they hadn't spoken, and didn't even know who the other was, their hearts were set like the needles of twin compasses.

"Who is she, teacher?" Rama asked the holy man.

The holy man hid his smile and answered, "Princess Sita, of course."

"May I meet her?" Rama thought if only he could hear her lovely voice he would be content for the rest of his days.

The holy man shook his head. "Unlikely. She is her father's precious pearl. Many, many princes from around the world have come to ask the king for her hand. But he will not even let one of them near her unless they can pass the test he has set for the man who will be worthy of her."

"Test?" Rama brightened. "What test?"

"Oh," the holy man lamented. "A very difficult one."

Rama and Lakshmana grew excited. They were beginning to enjoy difficult things. "Tell us," Lakshmana said.

"If any man would seek to marry beautiful Sita, he must first string the bow of Lord Shiva."

"Lord Shiva's bow?" Rama repeated.

"It fell to earth here when Shiva did battle in the heavens. Janak keeps it as a sign of the god's protection. But the bow is enormous. Every prince who has come to try cannot even manage to lift it, much less bend it to fit the string."

"So it is an impossible test?" Lakshmana said.

The holy man considered. "Some tests are meant only to show what cannot ever be done. But those tests are not true. A true test is meant to reveal what wonderful thing *can* be done when the right person comes along. They are meant to show something about the person, not the challenge itself."

"What kind of test is this one, then?" Rama asked.

The holy man pretended to hesitate. "Let's go and find out."

At the palace, Sita's father was impressed with the princes' regal bearing. And when he learned Rama and Lakshmana were the sons of Dasaratha, he was even more pleased. If anyone would take his daughter from his side, he hoped it would be one of these fine young men.

When Sita saw who had come to seek her hand, her heart leaped. But it fell just as quickly into despair. She knew the test to bend Shiva's bow was impossible.

But Rama was not discouraged. When he saw the bow, it seemed to call out to him, like he was meant to find it, like it was *dharma*. "Would you like to try first, Lakshmana?"

Lakshmana cracked a small smile. He could see

how smitten his brother was. He'd already made up his mind not to try—his brother's happiness meant more to him than any test. "You go first, brother."

Relieved, Rama reached out and picked up the bow as easily as a panther might scoop up her cub in her jaw. He set the bow on its end, braced it with his legs, and reached up with the looped end of the string.

What happened next shocked everyone. Rama not only succeeded in bending the bow that no one else had so much as been able to budge, but he also broke it clean in half!

The king was amazed. Sita was overjoyed. Lakshmana nearly burst with pride. Rama was thrilled. Only the holy man was unsurprised by this turn of events, and he kept himself to himself, smiling quietly as Rama and Sita were at last allowed to meet and the kingdom flew into a frenzy of preparation for the royal wedding.

Four days flit by. With every passing lunchtime and every late evening in the garden, Ram becomes more apprentice than unwanted employee. Nek has begun a new statue, but the process is slow. The first day, they bound pieces of construction rod with twine to make a stick figure. The second, they covered the frame in chicken wire, bending and roughing out the form. The third, Ram tore and soaked newspaper into strips that Nek wrapped over the frame. The fourth saw them adding more wire, more wet newspaper.

The nights have been long, but Ram is happier

than he's ever been. Too happy and keyed up to sleep when he climbs back to his rooftop bed. The parades don't help much either, more frequent and louder than ever as they pass through the street below. And it is turning cold, the season sliding toward winter.

Saturday morning Ram shivers under his blanket and snatches at sleep like a monkey picking fleas. Finally he gives up and goes down to the street. At least Nek only has to work the morning and not the whole day. At least they'll have the entire afternoon and evening to work on the next stage for the statue, the one Ram's been most looking forward to: molding the cement onto the wire-and-newspaper skeleton.

And there'll be plenty of time for a story, he thinks. He's been learning so much and been so focused on the work that he's forgotten to ask what happened next to the two brothers and Sita.

At the end of Ram's alley, the street is littered with the remnants of last night's parade. Spent firecrackers. Paper wrappers. Wilted marigold petals.

"Ram!" Daya shouts from the corner in front of her father's building. "Hey, Ram!"

He hasn't seen her since the rickshaw ride. She

runs to him, dressed not in her school uniform but in a pair of red pants and a bulky woolen sweater. Ram eyes the sweater with envy. Daya misreads his gaze and scratches at her neck. "Maa made me wear this today. It isn't even that cold out. And this thing is so itchy." Ram needs to find something warm to wear soon. How nice would it be to have someone just hand him a fresh new sweater, itchy or no? Last year he found a good one under the bench at the play field, where a careless boy had shed it when the chilly morning gave way to a warmer day. It was only a little small, and Ram wore holes in it by the time the spring rains came. "C'mon. There are so many kids in the park. Papa says I can—"

"Not now, Daya."

He's halfway to the factory before Daya understands that he has said no. She runs to catch up. "But, Ram," she says. "I've been waiting. We can go and hit—"

He must have slept later than he realized. The factory gate is already locked tight. Nek's bicycle is not parked inside. He must already be at the garden.

"I'm busy today, Daya. Maybe tomorrow. Or Monday. You don't have school on Monday, do you?"

"Busy?" Daya makes a face. "Don't you even want to know where I've been? Why I haven't been around?"

She waits. Ram realizes it has been almost a week since he last saw her. "Vijay and those boys are really mad. They're looking for you. And they've been following me after school. I've led them on silly routes until I finally just go home. He wants that dumb watch back," Daya says.

"I heard him that day at the school. Bothering you. I'm sorry, Daya."

"They're all *bewakoofs*. But I've been protecting you by *not* coming here, and now that I finally got here, you are too *busy*?"

Ram feels terrible. "I'm sorry, Daya. Here—" He starts to undo the clasp on the watch, but she sighs.

"No," she says. "I'm not giving it back. You won it, fair and square, and they won't hurt me. But you need to be careful, Ram."

"Thanks, Daya," Ram is more relieved than he is willing to admit. He's grown attached to the watch. And giving in to Peach Fuzz would be awful. "I'll find you tomorrow, *changa*?"

He starts to run.

"Ram!" Ram stops. Daya is following him. He

notices the paper bag for the first time. "Here," she says, voice defiant, but eyes soft like he's the one yelling at her. "I saved these for you."

He peeks in the bag. *Pakoras.* The cheese kind. "Thanks."

"Let me run and ask Papa if I can go with you—"

"No!" Ram says quickly, snatching the bag.

"But Ram—"

"I can't wait," Ram says by way of excuse. "We'll hit *gilli* soon."

Daya plants a fist on her hip. "Tomorrow."

"I promise," Ram says. "*Changa fer?*"

Daya only shrugs and walks sullenly back to her father's office.

Ram runs to the corner, and then all the way to the garden.

When he arrives, Nek is finishing his lunch.

"I brought food, too," Ram says, shaking the sack at him. Nek waves him off. "Eat them yourself. I thought you weren't coming, so I ate your portion already."

"Oh." Good thing Ram loves *pakoras*. He reaches into his bag. They are cold, but still crunchy in spots and good and greasy in the middle.

Nek repacks his lunch things, and then pulls

three twenty-rupee coins from his pocket. "Your wages."

Ram grins. "My winnings."

"Call them what you will," Nek says without looking at him. "You earned them."

Nek returns to mixing cement as Ram studies the coins. He is pleased to have some of his money back, but struck by how he'd almost forgotten about the bargain.

Somehow this fact pleases him even more than the money itself.

"Let me help." Ram stuffs another *pakora* into his mouth.

Nek keeps working. "You can do the next batch."

Ram studies the statue. He notices for the first time that this one doesn't have two legs like the others; instead the chicken wire forms a long, full sweep at the bottom. Like a skirt.

"It's Sita, isn't it?" he says.

Nek sits back. "Very good."

"You haven't told me yet what happened after they got married."

Nek stops mixing. "You're right. But I think it is time for you to tell a story. How did you come to Chandigarh?"

"I have always been here."

"Alone?"

"Not always. There was a girl once." The bead burns at his chest. He wonders if he should show it to Nek. The man knows something about art. Or at least about making things.

But no.

"Was she kind to you?"

Ram conjures the girl's face. "Yes." She used to sing to him, that he remembers. He even remembers her telling him stories, but not the stories themselves. Only the safe feeling of listening to her voice in the darkness. Did she tell him Rama's tales? She must have. Maybe that's why the story sometimes feels familiar.

His heart twists and crunches down when he thinks of her, though he is not sure why. "She was very pretty. And not old. She was much taller than I was. I called her Pehn."

"*Pehn* means sister."

Ram lifts a shoulder. He only knows it is what he called her, not if it was truly who she was. She treated him like a mother would a son. "It was long ago. When I was littler."

"How little?"

Ram has had five festival seasons—five seasons

of parades and pageants and fireworks—since he saw the girl last.

"Maybe seven years old," Ram says.

Nek makes a little noise and adds water to the cement. "Where did she go?"

Ram screws up his face. "She told me one day that a nice man offered her a good job in a big house. She was happy. And she told me that she would have money for us soon. That we might even have money to share a room with beds and windows and everything. A big black car took her away."

Nek's voice sounds funny as he asks, "Did she say what kind of job?"

"Does it matter?" Ram asks. "What kind of job?"

Nek's smile is less convincing than the ones his laughing soldiers wear. "Probably not."

Singh had acted and sounded just like this when Ram told him about Pehn.

"I'll find her someday," Ram says now, just as he once said to Singh.

Nek doesn't reply.

"When I have enough money, I'll buy my own *tuk-tuk*, maybe even a car, and search for her."

Nek wipes a hand over his chin. "That would be

a good end to that story," he says after too long. His voice sounds funny.

Ram still has three *pakoras* left, but he's not so hungry anymore. The breeze shushes through the rosewood leaves.

Then Nek, his voice still funny but trying to sound gruff, says, "Concrete's getting dry. Her sari will be ready for decorating soon."

"Decorated with what? More broken pots?"

"Broken pots won't do for Sita." He pops up and fetches a box from the supply tarp. Ram knows from the sound that it is the bangles. "These."

Nek looks at Ram expectantly, waiting for him to figure it out.

Ram knows—*feels*—he is being tested. Nek wants to see what he will do. Nek wants to see if Ram can see as he sees.

And Ram knows it is a true test, just like the one Rama faced with Shiva's bow.

Ram pulls one of the smashed bangles from the box, holds it up to the statue. He unfolds it enough to slip it over Sita's arm.

Too big.

He crimps it around her wrist.

Too bulky.

He balances it on top of her head, like a crown. Too silly.

Nek pretends to busy himself tidying up the shop, but then Ram spies a pair of snips in a wooden tool-box. He grabs them and cuts the bangle at the weak points where it was bent before. Then he holds the fragments up against the statue, bending the ends back easily.

He almost gasps when he sees it, what he figures Nek was imagining all along: those bangles, broken and cut and rearranged, will make a pattern more beautiful and colorful than any sari in the whole world.

"It will take a while," Nek says without turning. "But it will be worth it."

Ram drops to the dirt, too happy to have passed to care how long it will take, or how sore his hands will grow.

15

When they leave the garden together late that afternoon, Nek rides home, but Ram feels energized by what he's accomplished. Sita is taking shape. The chicken-wire-newspaper frame is done, and cement covers the skirt up to her waist. Nek showed Ram how to smooth it with his hands.

Ram doesn't want to go back to his sector yet. And it's been ages since he last took a bath. Now his usual grime is layered over with cement and grease and smoke. It is time. And the lake is just south of the garden.

He hurries past the wide boardwalk on the front

side of the lake, crowded with walkers even at this time of day. He picks along the shore opposite the docks, deeper into the marshy parts where there are no paths. When he reaches his favorite spot, he strips down and steps into the chilly water. Ram likes being clean, but he wishes it didn't have to be so cold. He finds the cake of soap he hid under some rocks the last time he bathed and lathers as best he can. If it were warmer and earlier, he'd wash his clothes, too, but not tonight. How nice it would be to have clean clothes waiting for him when he came out of the bath. He knows other kids must have taps in their homes, and towels to dry off with rather than just the weak sunlight and the breeze to shiver in. But Rama and Lakshmana didn't have warm water or clean tubs on their adventures. Ram takes some pride in that they had to bathe in forest streams and lakes like this one.

The watch on his wrist feels funny in the water, and for a moment Ram panics. The he remembers that it is waterproof. Good. He holds it up to catch the light.

Siyappa!

A great glob of concrete has crusted around the buttons on the left side. And the little display is blank instead of filled with the numbers and the date.

He tries all the buttons. Nothing. No sound at all. *Hoye.*

Ram emerges from the water, staring at the ruined watch. Maybe from concrete, or maybe Peach Fuzz lied about it being waterproof. Either way, Ram is more heartbroken than he cares to admit. Maybe it will dry out and work again. He can only hope.

Ram dresses and wanders back to town, invisible in the way only a boy like Ram can be. He plucks an orange from another shrine to Rama and Sita, this one with the two lovers holding hands and facing each other.

How could Lord Rama secretly carry so much of Lord Vishnu and not even have known it himself? How could something so wonderful be hidden from everyone? And how is it possible Ram shares a name with such a man as this? Did Rama ever feel invisible?

Ram passes the small play field attached to the government school. He wonders: If Rama could hold such secrets, maybe he can too.

Maybe, he thinks, *I am secretly a prince.* He would not be so greedy as to aspire to being a god, but a prince? Why not? Or if not a prince, at least the lost son of a wealthy man who laid a full table every night. *Or maybe the lost son of an artist who marked you with a special bead before you were separated.*

Ram is embarrassed by his imagination. Nonsense. Besides, Pehn gave him the bead.

But who gave it to Pehn? Of course it couldn't have been Nek. But still. The notion burrows down inside his mind and takes root, like a weed growing out of the sidewalk.

Alongside it grows another idea. Maybe Ram and Nek were supposed to meet. Maybe they were meant to look after each other. Like Rama and Lakshmana.

Maybe Ram doesn't have to be quite so alone.

There are a dozen kids playing *pithoo* in an area where the grass is worn down to nubs, dust clouding around them with every step. Ram leans against the fence. He's played before, but he's not very good. *Pithoo* requires friends to play with you.

A girl his own age knocks down the tower of stones and begins running, another boy rushing up to restack them while another kid chases the girl, throws the ball, and tags her out.

A little farther on he sees another game going.

Cricket. Yes. A little cricket would be fine. And if the cricket evolves into a *gilli* match, a little wager, well, his pockets and his stomach will not say no.

Ram climbs the fence and begins jogging toward the boys. He's maybe fifty yards away when the bowler stops, takes a few steps, and points at Ram. *Good,* Ram is relieved. *They want me to join in!*

But the tallest calls out to the others, and as one they move toward him. Ram is frozen for a second, losing precious time. Something isn't right.

The pack comes into sharper focus. Peach Fuzz glares at Ram just as murderously as the day Ram took his watch. "It's him!"

Ram's so dumbstruck by his bad luck that he remains fixed to the spot. Or maybe it wasn't just bad luck. Maybe they were in this end of town for a reason, looking for him. When following Daya didn't work, maybe they figured coming to the area where they lost track of him would. Either way, Ram can't believe it. The broken watch feels like a weight on his wrist.

The boys are closing fast, and he is in an open field with nowhere to hide. Finally his legs remember what to do, and he runs.

Ram's toes find holds in the chain-link fence and he throws himself over and breaks into a sprint. Too soon he hears the pack hitting the fence as well, rattling it as they climb over like some many-armed monster.

He's still in the open, still exposed. He could run back toward his own sector, but he's led them there once, and if they see that, they'll know where to find him for certain.

The forest. He can hide in the forest.

He veers right, hard and quick, feet slipping on something slimy, but he keeps moving. Ahead he can see the new road the city is building. He hurdles over the dirt piled up at the edges, feet kicking up the gravel waiting to be paved over with smooth blacktop. On the other side, he leaps again, launching into the trees.

It swallows him up. A clutch of hoopoes shriek *oop-oop-oop* and scatter as Ram charges deeper in. He can still hear the boys shouting behind him, though he is uncertain if they have followed him inside. He has stuck to the paths around the workshop, and this part of the forest is unfamiliar. The cover is denser and the light is lower.

Ram trips over a scrubby neem tree, its yellow berries squishing under his feet. He must hide. Another banyan tree, maybe, where he can wait for the boys to give up.

But then his knee explodes in a fireball of pain. A sound like the shattering of a hundred stones fills the air, and for a moment Ram wonders if it is the sound of a bone breaking. He draws the knee up to his chest and hops wildly on the other foot, biting his bottom lip, fighting against the urge to cry out.

Then he sees what he hit.

Siyappa! A statue lies on its side. One hand holds something like a pitchfork. Miraculously, the pitchfork's spindly tines have survived the fall, but the head has rolled a few feet away, one eye dislodged from its socket. But what is one of Nek's statues doing all the way out here? And if it is out here, are there others nearby as well? Is he closer to the garden than he thought? Or is the garden much bigger than he realized?

Suddenly Ram is not worried about the boys anymore—he is worried about Nek. What will Nek say? Ram limps toward the head, hoping against hope that he can just put it back on and Nek won't know the difference. But two steps closer he goes still.

Just beyond where the head has fallen, the ground drops away, a gorge some twenty feet deep and sixty feet long opening up below him. It is sheer on both sides, with only scrubby bushes filling in the bottom. Ram could have launched himself over that cliff. He could have been hurt far worse than just a banged-up knee. He looks at the fallen statue, feeling oddly like the thing has saved him, has sacrificed itself for him.

Ram scoops up the head, backing away from the precipice. He positions it near the body and tries to imagine how he will tell Nek.

Behind him, he can hear the boys calling to one another. They are closer.

"He went in there!"

"Go after him!"

"*You* go after him!"

They are afraid of the forest. But their fear won't keep them back for long.

"Spread out and search!" Ram can recognize the voice of Peach Fuzz now. What's more, he can tell that they are closer.

If they keep coming, they'll find the statue.

He has to draw them away.

Ram leaves the statue where it has fallen and begins crashing through the brush, making as much noise as he can as he cuts toward the new road that dead-ends into the one the boys chased him across. Just to make sure they take the bait, he calls out as loud as he can, "Little schoolboys afraid of the forest?"

The taunt hits the mark.

"He's heading east toward the main sector!"

"We'll get him now!"

Ram tries to enjoy the fact that his plan is working, but his knee is slowing him down. Plus, it's easier for the boys to keep pace with him as they run along the edge of the forest. They'll be even with him by the time he is in the open again.

Faster.

He makes it to the road and vaults over the earthen embankments, springing past the piles of stones.

"There he is!"

Ram doesn't dare glance back. He ignores the pain in his knee, but his lungs are beginning to burn. He can't keep up this pace. . . .

At his own sector, he rounds the corner and sees his salvation. Another of the processions is clogging the lane. Giant paper heads, cars covered with garlands of marigolds and jasmine, horses bearing handsome men and women. A large battery of drummers keeps time, an army of horn players and bell ringers following behind. The cars honk as voices chant.

Ram dives into the thicket of musicians and horses' legs, running with the flow of the parade as he goes. A man reaches over from his horse as if to swat him, but for the most part, no one pays Ram much mind. He runs all the way to the beginning of the procession, passes under a platform borne on the shoulders of four men.

Only after he dives into the crowd on the opposite side of the street does he pause to look back.

No sign of the boys.

And then he sees what those men were carrying on the platform: life-size plaster figures of Rama and Sita, their hands raised in blessing.

As Lord Rama passes, Ram cannot help but notice the little smirk someone has painted on his face.

And Ram smiles back.

17

The next morning, Ram doesn't feel like he has slept at all. He also doesn't feel much like eating. He lingers at the corner for Daya before figuring out that it is Sunday. Even though he knows Nek is probably already at the garden, he stalls. He finds some kids hitting *gilli* in a park in Sector 13 and picks up a few rupees. But he hits badly, the sound of the sticks cracking together too much like the snap of the statue's neck.

He still isn't ready to face Nek, so he settles in to watch part of a pageant play in the park. Thanks to Nek's story, Ram recognizes the characters, but he is too far away to make out what the actors are saying. Even still, the holiday season is all beginning to make sense. The endless parades and overflowing shrines and pageants are part of this story. It makes him feel wise to know about how things connect.

But he can't shake the worry—the worry of what Nek will say when he explains what happened last night. By the time he finally makes his way to the workshop, the worry sits heavy, like Ram has swallowed stones.

"Where have you been?" Nek says. He's already adding the next layer of cement to Sita's form.

"I have to show you something, Uncle ji."

Nek doesn't glance up. "What is it?"

"Er," he begins. "There is a statue I ran into last night."

Nek stops smoothing out the cement. "Ran into?"

Ram nods. "It was an accident. It was dark, and I didn't know that part of the forest and I broke it." He says, repeating, "By accident."

"Where?" Nek growls.

Ram gestures into the thicket. "That way. I don't know how far. At the top of a sort of ravine—"

Nek is already walking, quicker than Ram has seen him move before.

Ram hurries to catch up.

Nek's silence is unbearable. Ram follows him along an almost invisible path through the trees. They pass through another arched doorway, the wall extending ten feet or so on either side, covered in bits of broken mirror. A little farther on, they pass by the exposed roots of a tree as the hillside towers over the path. Only on his second look does Ram realize that the roots are not real roots. They are made of cement, though how Nek has managed to make them twist and curve this way Ram cannot guess.

"Why is it so far away?" Ram asks finally. "From the other statues?"

Nek does not slow down. "Shiva is where he is supposed to be."

"Shiva?" Ram asks. The one whose bow Rama lifted? Why does he belong here and not with the laughing army?

They hurry on. From the dry streambed on their left comes the *chit-chit-chit* of a mongoose, and the answering hiss of a cobra. But Nek doesn't even slow down.

They reach the ravine Ram almost stumbled into last night. Nek climbs up the hillside, using the cement tree roots as handholds. The drop into the ravine is not as steep as Ram thought it was last night in the dark, but it still could have injured him badly.

When they reach the top, Nek goes straight to the spot and scoops up Shiva's head. Ram follows slowly. Nek's anger and frustration radiate off him in waves. "What were you doing up here? I told you not to be in the garden without me."

Ram can't believe how small his own voice sounds. "I didn't think I was. All the things you showed me in the garden are hundreds of meters from here."

Nek scans the ground. "Where is his eye?"

"I don't know, Uncle ji."

Nek crouches, begins combing the undergrowth for Shiva's lost eye. "You didn't even bother to search for it?"

"I didn't have time. . . ." Even now he stands paralyzed, fiddling with the strap of the broken watch.

Nek keeps searching. "You had time to creep around my garden when you were told not to, time to break Lord Shiva's head clean off, but not the time to find all the pieces?"

Ram's frustration boils into anger. "I didn't have time because I was being chased!"

Nek's hands go still. His voice is quiet, somehow even more terrifying. "Chased?"

"These boys, they chased me last week when I won their money. I ran into them yesterday half a kilometer from here and I thought I could hide in this section of the forest, but—"

"You led them here?" Nek is on his feet. He still holds Shiva's head in his hands. Ram worries he might throw it at him. "You led them *here*?"

"I didn't think they'd follow me. But they did. After I knocked over the statue, I realized they were still coming. So I made a lot of noise and led them back to the street and outran them back to my sector before I hid in a parade."

But Nek doesn't seem to have heard anything else. Doesn't care that Ram was clever, or quick, or that he got the boys to follow him away from the garden instead of deeper in.

"Leave," Nek says coldly.

"But—"

"Out!" Nek is transformed. Ram knew he would be angry, but he didn't expect this! He's been yelled at plenty of times, thrown out of shops and doorways often enough, but this is different. It was never a friend shouting or sending him away before.

"But I *saved* the garden . . . ," Ram begins. "I kept them from seeing it. And you still owe me money—"

"Go before I lose my temper!" Nek palms Shiva's head with one hand, points with the other back toward the road.

Ram is used to being unwanted. But being banished is new. And so much worse.

18

Ram stays away for four whole days. He spends them in distant sectors, making sure to come back late, after the factory is shut, so he won't risk running into Nek.

At dusk on Thursday, Ram slumps on the curb across from the municipal building with a few pieces of buttery naan from the tandoor past the market. He bought them with one of the coins Nek paid him with on Saturday. The bread tastes like paste in his mouth.

Somehow having had a job to do and now having it ripped away is the worst thing of all. When

Sita was just beginning to look real, too.

A burst of red explodes in the sky overhead, the boom coming a second later. The sky has barely begun to surrender to dusk, but the fireworks have already begun. They pop and hiss from all around him, sulfurous smoke clouding the air. They'll continue starting earlier and earlier, all the way up until the last day of the festival, until Dussehra ends and the three-week countdown to Diwali begins.

"Hello, Ram." Singh settles beside him, a few feet away.

"Why are you still here?"

"Catching up on some work."

A parade rounds the corner at the end of the lane and begins marching up the street. First a corps of drummers, then a motley assortment of people clanging cowbells and cymbals. A pair of trumpets bleat tunelessly.

"I looked for Daya today." He ignored her for so long that somehow not finding her seemed like another punishment he deserved.

"Her mother and grandmother took her to see some cousins in Ludhiana for a few days. They won't see each other at Diwali, so they exchange gifts now."

"Oh."

The parade creeps closer. "She's been missing you."

Ram shrugs. "I thought you didn't like her hanging around with me anyway."

Singh hesitates. "I don't like her gambling with you. Or for you. But she likes you. She doesn't have many friends at school."

Ram shrugs. "I was busy."

The parade fills the street. Behind the musicians, a group of young men pull another of the giant papier-mâché statues. This one has a dark brow and pointed teeth. Like last night, they'll carry it to the bonfire at the middle of the sector and burn it up. How the demon fits in with the story of Rama and Lakshmana and Sita, Ram isn't sure. Maybe it's the one they faced first in the jungle with the holy man? And he realizes with a pang that he may never have a chance to ask Nek.

"Busy," Singh repeats, interrupting his thoughts. "With the man with the bicycle?"

Ram remembers that Singh saw them together.

"Who is he, Ram?"

Ram fiddles with the broken watch buttons as he considers the question. Who is Nek? A factory worker. An artist. For a little while, Ram's friend.

He wouldn't even be that if he hadn't taken Ram's money in the first place—

Money.

A flame of anger flickers in Ram's chest. Nek hasn't even paid him back, not fully. And now Ram won't even be able to earn it back. It isn't fair. If only he'd beaten Nek that afternoon. Then he wouldn't be in this whole mess. He could have taken one of the statues and gotten something for it like he planned and saved himself a pile of trouble.

Then again, what's stopping him now?

"Do you still need art for your museum, Uncle ji?"

Singh is thrown by the change of subject. "The museum? We haven't even built it yet. Someday they will, but right now it's all committees trying to figure out what kind to put in—"

"But you'll have to buy the art, right?"

"Well, I suppose."

It would be simple, *so simple*, to just take one of Nek's statues. And the best part is Nek won't even be able to say anything about it, since he's not supposed to be using the land or making all those statues in the first place.

Ram is careful to sound disinterested. "Is art expensive?"

"Sometimes. Some of the people on the museum committee want to fill the completed building with European paintings, to show how modern we are. Those paintings cost many, many lakh."

Lakh! A fraction of that would be enough for a bicycle, even a *tuk-tuk*. Enough to go searching for the girl.

"How do you know how much art is worth?"

"That's hard to say. Expense and worth are rarely the same thing."

"What does that mean?"

Singh gestures to Ram's neck. "Your bead. Someone made that. Someone with skill. And beyond that, it matters to you because of how you came to it. It is art of a kind. If someone offered you what it was worth, say a few paisa, would you take it?"

"No."

Singh nods. "Because its value to you is greater than what someone says it is worth to them. And India is full of that kind of craftsmanship. Fancy paintings are fine, but they're only one kind of art. And there is plenty to be found right here in the Punjab that is just as wonderful." He pauses, points at the effigies heading toward the bonfire. "Even those. See how the life seeps up through them. The care and the artistry. That's the art of this place. Not some painting from a hundred years ago of a French countryside."

Ram shrugs. "But they're just going to burn it up."

"True. But it doesn't mean it isn't art. It doesn't mean it doesn't matter. Remember how I told you I liked to draw when I was a boy?"

Ram nods.

"I made effigies, too. With my friends. I spent weeks working on them. And then at Dussehra my friends and I would fill them with firecrackers and blow them up. And after we'd blown them up, we'd ride over the pieces on our bicycles." Singh's eyes shine at the memory.

"Seems like a lot of trouble just to celebrate a stupid love story."

Singh looks at him sharply. "Love story?"

Ram finally meets his eye. "Rama and Sita. Getting married. I know about it."

"You think all this . . ." Singh waves toward the parade passing by, trails off. "Tell me what you know about the story, Ram."

Ram tells him what Nek has told him. About King Dasaratha. The births of the brothers. How close Rama and Lakshmana were. The holy man. Slaying the demon. Bending the bow. Winning Sita's hand.

"Happily ever after, I guess," Ram finishes. How dull it all sounds now. A magical birth, an obstacle to happiness easily overcome. Really, why did Ram even care what happened next?

"You're only coming to the good part," Singh says, his face more relaxed than Ram has ever seen it. "The most important part."

19

After Rama and Sita's wedding, the holy man decided it was time to go back to Ayodhya.

Their reception at the palace put the wedding to shame. They feasted for days, the entire kingdom celebrating the return of the two princes, and Rama so well married. When the festivities at last began to quiet, the king made a decision.

Dasaratha decided to pass his kingdom on to one of his sons when he still had strength left to advise and guide the new king.

It was obvious to all that Rama was the perfect heir. And now with Sita at his side and his adventures behind him, he was ready to rule.

But Kaikeyi—Dasaratha's youngest wife—feared what might happen if Rama were named king. As the youngest of the wives, she'd always been jealous of the love Dasaratha showed to Kausalya, and of the way *everyone* preferred Rama to her own son, Bharata. Kaikeyi's heart was small and cold, and she could only imagine that Rama would toss her and her son out of the palace if he came to power. So she prevailed upon the king to deliver on a pledge he had made to her many years ago.

"Do you recall, King Dasaratha," she said one evening, "that you promised me two wishes?"

The king nodded. "Of course. One when you saved my life in battle, and the other when you agreed to become my wife."

"And you recall that I have not asked you for those wishes, in all these many years we have been wed?"

"Yes."

"I ask for them now." She drew herself up, her face grim.

Now King Dasaratha grew worried. The timing

of her request . . . just as he prepared to name his heir . . .

"Kaikeyi—"

"I wish for Bharata to be king instead of Rama!"

The king hid his face in his hands and wept. "Please, Kaikeyi—"

"Besides, Bharata will make a fine king." She did not go so far as to say he would make a *better* king than Rama. Not even she believed that.

Honor and duty bound, Dasaratha had to comply. He took solace in the fact that Rama, as noble and generous as he was, would not mind being passed over. He would, after all, still be in Ayodhya, on hand to advise his brother.

"Very well," the king replied. "Bharata will be the king."

But Kaikeyi knew that if Rama remained in the kingdom, even her own son would defer to him, knew that others would insist he be made king. Her fear made her second wish even more devastating than her first. "You will also banish Rama from the kingdom for a span of fourteen years."

"Kaikeyi! No!"

But the young queen was unmoved by her husband's pleas, unmoved by his heartbreak.

"A promise is a promise," she said. "And any man—especially a king—is nothing without his word."

So it was that the very next morning, Dasaratha announced that Bharata would be named king and that Rama would be banished for fourteen years.

All of Ayodhya mourned, even Bharata, who had no desire to be king, especially under these circumstances. The other queens wept openly. Even the holy man was confused and worried. He had not foreseen this.

Rama alone was at peace with the odd twist of fate. Perhaps he had grown to enjoy adventure and traveling and the wilds of the jungle. Or perhaps he was as happy to obey his father's will as anyone could ever be. Even Bharata could not convince him to stay.

"No, brother, it is my duty and my pleasure to fulfill my father's obligation. I will live in the jungle for fourteen years."

But he would not go alone.

"I will go with you, husband," Sita said.

"As will I," said Lakshmana.

Rama was overwhelmed by their kindness, but he could not ask them to join his exile. "No, you both must stay. A hard life in the jungle is no substitute for life in the palace. This is your home."

"My home is with you, Rama," Sita replied.

"And I will not stay behind growing fat and comfortable while there are dangers to face and adventures to be had." Lakshmana was fierce enough that not even Rama himself would argue with him.

So Rama agreed.

The entire kingdom gathered at the river to see them off. Bharata reluctantly let them go, but not before making an important gesture. "Give me your sandals, Rama," he ordered. "They will sit on the throne—not me—as a symbol of your rightful place as king. I rule only in your stead for these fourteen years."

Rama embraced Bharata. As Rama, Sita, and Lakshmana climbed into the boat to cross the river,

the holy man made as if to follow. Rama saw the
man was weary, and fourteen years in the wilderness would not treat the sage well. He placed a hand
on his teacher's shoulder. "Please," he said. "Stay
behind. Advise my brother Bharata. Teach him as
you have taught me and Lakshmana."

The holy man, humbled and surprised by Rama's
character and generosity, agreed to do what he
could.

And so it was that Rama, Sita, and Lakshmana left
the kingdom, striking out once again into the wilds
and dangers of the great jungle.

By the time Singh finishes the telling, the parade has passed. "So Rama left? Just like that?"

"Yes," Singh says.

"Sita had to go with him since she was his wife, right?" Ram asks.

"Well, I suppose that—"

"But Lakshmana gave up an easy life in a great palace," Ram says.

"It is hard to believe. But that's what true friends do. Life in exile is nothing when you have at least one true friend at your side."

Ram considers the word. Exile. Once again, he

thinks he knows how Rama must have felt—pushed out of a place he loved. Only it wasn't Rama's fault. It was Kaikeyi's for being jealous, and Dasaratha's for making stupid promises.

Ram, however, has only himself to blame for his own exile. But if he is responsible, then maybe he is the one who can make it right, too.

He rises to his feet.

"*Shukriya*, Uncle ji," he says.

"Don't you want to hear what happens next?"

Ram does. Dearly. But what he has to do should not wait.

"I have to go and talk to someone."

Singh's voice flattens out again. "Your friend?"

"Yes." Nek *is* his friend. Or was. Or maybe can be again.

"Just be wise, Ram," Singh says, then adds carefully, "People are not always what they seem. Sometimes grown people pretend to be good to children. . . ."

"I'm all right, Uncle ji."

"It's just . . ." Singh struggles for the words. "The girl. The one who gave you your bead? She trusted the man who took her away, didn't she?"

Ram doesn't see what this has to do with him or Nek.

"I can take care of myself, Uncle ji."

Singh sighs. "Sometimes I wish you didn't have to."

Ram isn't sure what that means.

"Did you ever think of having a home?"

Ram makes a face. "I'm not going back to that orphanage."

"I know. But . . . what if my wife agreed to let you share the houseboy's room? We could find some jobs for you. We could see that you go to school—"

Ram shakes his head and backs away.

"No, thank you, Uncle ji," he says quickly. But his heart swells with the kindness of the offer. A place to live and food and living near—if not with—Singh and Daya would be nice. School might not even be so awful.

But not working in a house.

Pehn went to a big house to work.

Singh smiles sadly. "Yes. I thought so. But if you change your mind . . ."

"Good-bye, Uncle ji." Ram starts toward the garden.

The street is a mess again. But in among all the trash something glints brightly. Ram dashes over. A saffron-colored *dupatta*, covered in perfectly round mirrors. He scoops the scarf up. Maybe it will be useful. If only Nek will forgive him.

When Ram at last reaches the clearing, Nek is working on a new statue. A bear, he realizes at once. Sita sits nearby, frozen the way she was when Ram worked last.

Nek glances up, but he doesn't send Ram away.

Ram takes a few steps closer, holds out the *dupatta*. "I found this."

Nek surveys the mirrors. "Found or stole?"

"Found. In the road after a parade."

Nek adds more cement. "We don't steal to make things. Only what we find. What no one else wants."

Ram is too pleased to speak. Nek said *we*.

"I know."

Nek glances at the scarf. His hands are dabbed with wet cement. "Put it with the bangles. You can continue cutting them when we get back."

"Back from where?" Ram tosses the scarf onto the bangle box. Has Nek forgiven him this easily? It almost makes him more nervous, the uncertainty.

"Back from fixing Shiva." He stands, picks up a bucket. "Bring a torch."

They take the same path back up through the forest. Nek pauses at a tree covered in mottled red-and-gray bark. He heaves a stone up through the spread of waxy green leaves and rouses a chorus of chattering, growling langurs. A second later three or four yellow gooseberries zip toward them as the monkeys jump from the branches. Nek gathers up the little yellow fruit and offers them to Ram.

"You can eat these?"

"Yes."

Ram takes a bite. The bitter, biting juice explodes in his mouth.

Nek's grin comes and goes like a wink. "Of course they are better after you stew them in salt and chili powder."

Ram spits out the sour, stringy mess and chucks

the rest of the berries into the forest as they walk on.

From the bottom of the ravine, Nek points to the rim. "This will be a waterfall. That is why Shiva is up there. All alone."

Waterfall? All Ram sees are trees and shadow, rivulets of bare dirt where the rain has washed into the gully.

"Someday I will make this whole hillside into a great cascade. I've already drawn up the plans for the cisterns and the pumps and the piping."

"You know how to do that?" Ram asks. "Dig wells and build pumps?"

Nek climbs up, the bucket dangling from one arm. "I grew up on a farm, remember? I dug wells with the men in the village. We piped water to the fields. It is not so hard. But I haven't found all the pieces yet."

For a moment, Ram can see it as Nek does—a wall of water coursing down this hillside. It will be beautiful. Then he follows him up the roots.

"But why does Shiva need a waterfall?"

"Waterfalls are the hair of the Lord Shiva. Shiva is the destroyer, pushing all things toward destruction so that they can be reborn. The way water cleans and transforms what it touches."

At the top, the broken statue has been righted,

the head sitting beside it. "So Shiva knows a thing or two about destroying. You have that in common at least." Ram winces at the jab. "But I suspect you are also a rebuilder. Like him."

"I really didn't mean to, Uncle ji."

"I know," Nek says. "And Shiva doesn't mind. He did worse." Nek hands the bucket of mortar to Ram and picks up the head.

"Is he in the *Ramayana* too?" Ram asks.

"In a way. But not this part. *Oye*, Ram," he sighs, "I need a thousand statues to tell you all the stories you must know."

"Tell me this one."

"Shiva had a wife named Parvati. While he was off dancing on top of the globe, destroying and rebuilding, Parvati grew lonely. One day, she'd had enough of loneliness. So she took some turmeric paste and mud and mixed it together, sculpting a beautiful baby boy out of the clay. Using her own magic (she was a goddess after all), she breathed life into the baby. She called him Ganesha."

Nek pauses, jerks his chin at the headless statue. "Work and listen."

Ram smears wet concrete on top of the broken neck.

"Years later, Lord Shiva returned. At the moment he happened upon the house, Parvati was bathing, and little Ganesha was standing guard outside the door. Shiva, of course, had no idea who the boy was, and was annoyed when Ganesha would not let him inside the house. And so Shiva the destroyer lost his temper. In haste, he drew his sword and sliced off the head of the insolent little boy in one clean blow."

Ram's hands go still. *Cut off his boy's head?* The concrete plops from his fingers before he remembers what he's doing and resumes buttering the edges. "That's awful!"

"Shiva regretted his action at once. But was he not also the rebuilder? He dashed into the forest and found a young elephant that had lost his mother. Shiva removed the elephant calf's head and hurried back."

"He did *what*?"

"Don't interrupt," Nek says. "Then he did as we are doing—only with magic instead of concrete. He restored both boy and elephant in one body."

At this, Nek reaches up with the head, nestles it into place. "Run your finger around the edge and smooth it out."

Ram obeys, but he can't believe what he's just heard. "That's a terrible story!" he exclaims.

Nek pulls his hands away gently. The head stays in place. He holds the torch up to inspect the seam. "Maybe. What happened is terrible. But what resulted was good. Destroyed. Rebuilt. That is the way of things."

And Ram understands that Nek is apologizing, too. In his own way.

Nek shines the light at the ground, scans the undergrowth. "Do you see where his eye has fallen?"

Ram drops down; they search for a few minutes before Ram sighs, shines the light back at Shiva. "I will make him another," Nek says. "Until then, he can wink at us."

Ram tries to laugh at the humor, but he's uneasy. Maybe the eye flew into the ravine? But if Nek isn't worried, why should Ram be?

With the light haloed around Shiva, Ram can see how magnificent the statue really is. The detail is intricate, the helmet on top of Shiva's head rising to a point as fine as a pencil's tip. He is free of the adornment of the soldiers, no broken tile armoring his body—just finely worked concrete shaped into muscle, clothing. It is better than anything Ram has seen elsewhere in the garden, better than anything he has ever seen in the city, even.

"Let's get back to Sita," Nek says, giving Shiva one last pat.

Ram follows, but his mind stays with Shiva up on the imaginary waterfall. Then it travels to the winding path and under the curving wall to the laughing army. And then to the menagerie and the village and who knows what else Nek has hidden out here.

"Why?" he asks, without realizing at first that he is speaking aloud.

"Why what?"

"Why go to all the trouble of making something so well only to hide it where no one can see it?"

"You have seen it."

Ram is almost annoyed. He suspects Nek knows what he means. Seen by people who matter, who know about statues and stories and all the things that Nek is bringing to life. Not a nobody like him. "I mean everyone. Don't you want to show off how good they are?"

They reenter the clearing and the workshop. "Other people don't have to see them for me to know they are special."

"But—"

"I do these things because I have to. Because if I don't, I cannot live with myself. That is the only way I can explain. And if others saw them, they would take it all away from me. I'm nothing. A man who works in a bicycle factory. A man who has claimed land that does not belong to him. If I show people what I have done, what do you think will happen?"

Ram realizes that Nek was more frightened than he was angry when he banished him. Ram brought the boys so close to discovering the garden. He could have ended it all!

"Back to work," Nek announces.

Ram studies Sita. Nek hasn't changed or added a single thing on her since Ram left. Four days and he hasn't done anything more on the statue they began together.

Nek waited. For him. Ram blinks. Hard. Nek waited for *him*.

"I need to finish Jambavan here first." Nek gestures to the bear. "But you can cut the bangles into pieces. With any luck, we might start placing them before I leave for Diwali week after next."

Leave for Diwali? Nek was leaving? Not now, just when they are friends again! "How long will you be gone, Uncle ji?" Ram asks casually, as if he doesn't care, not at all.

"Three days."

Three days. What will Ram do with himself?

Nek clears his throat. "Maybe if I show you how, you will want to come and work on the pattern. While I'm gone?"

"But you said—"

"I know what I said. But that was before."

"Yes!" Ram says quickly. "I will! I'll put the pieces just right. You'll see."

Nek seems satisfied. "Good."

Ram bends to his task, happy to be back at work, his joy growing with every snip.

Ram and Nek settle into a comfortable rhythm.
Nearly two weeks go by. The city explodes in
fireworks and bonfires of the giant statues on Victory
Day at the end of Dussehra and then settles down
again to wait for Diwali, the holiday that closes out
the festival season.

Schools are closed and some offices, too, but Nek's
factory stays open, and he and Ram continue working in the garden every night. Jambavan the bear
is finished and placed with the other animals. He's
heavier than some of the others, but still surprisingly
light. They all look like solid stone, but the way Nek

builds them, around the wire and newspaper, makes them easier to carry. Still, Jambavan is big enough and round enough that it takes both of them.

They work a little more on clearing out the land around Shiva, hauling dirt by buckets until Ram's arms and back ache. And last night, they finished covering Sita with concrete. Tonight they'll start decorating her. Ram can hardly wait.

Daya is stationed at the corner when Ram makes his way to the street in the morning.

"C'mon," she orders. "Maa let me come with Papa today. Papa said we could go to the park as long as I don't gamble, but he didn't say anything about *you*—"

Ram is still shaking off sleep. "I need to get something to eat."

"Papa gave me money." Daya changes direction abruptly. "We can eat and then go to the park."

She grabs his hand and leads him to Rakesh's stand. The dancing school lady shakes out a rug into the street. Her windows, like all the others in town, are spotless. Many people have been putting out their lights—the little clay oil lamps they burn at night this time of year. They line the walls and terraces, warming the streets with their glow.

And people have been scrubbing their homes, cleaning out closets. Ram even found a nice wool blanket—the same one he saw the dancing school lady wearing over her shoulders one cold morning a couple of weeks ago—folded up and left on top of the dustbins in the alley. He couldn't believe she'd throw away such a treasure, but he was glad she had when he slept warmly under it last night.

Daya smiles sweetly at the dancing school lady. The woman nods back, avoiding Ram's eye.

"Hello, Princess Daya," Rakesh says. "Special for you today. Three for one."

"Three for one!"

"Business is slow," Rakesh says. "Too many people sharing sweets. And many of the workers are away on holiday."

"We'll take six," Daya says, holding out the money. Rakesh wraps the samosas in a square of newspaper. Daya refuses her change, and she and Ram eat as they walk to the park.

Ram looks over his shoulder at the factory. They close at noon today and will be closed for the next few days for the holiday. And Nek has his journey tomorrow, so today is Ram's last day to work with him before he goes.

But he has at least an hour or two to fill before Nek is done.

"Ram!" Daya sounds annoyed.

"Huh?"

"Were you even listening?"

Ram swallows. "What did you say?"

A monster game of tag is already in progress in the park.

"I asked what you wanted to do, but you were too busy trying to get a glimpse of your weird friend."

"Nek uncle isn't weird."

Daya huffs. "What do you do, anyway? I've seen you go to that stand of trees past the unfinished street—"

"You followed me?"

"Only to the edge of the sector," Daya says. "Papa would skin me if I left the sector without him or you to walk with me. What's so special in that forest?"

"Nothing," Ram says quickly.

"Does he live there?"

Ram is panicked. First the boys follow him there, now Daya knows. How much longer can he keep the secret?

There is nothing he can say. "Let's join the game."

They run all morning, stopping once or twice to hit a few rounds of *gilli*, picking up a little bit of money.

And it seems to make Daya forget about her questions, about Ram and Nek and the jungle. Even Ram forgets briefly, enjoying the game and laughter and having Daya at his side again.

But then the factory whistle blows. Ram glances at the watch out of habit, before remembering that it is broken.

"I have to go!"

Daya throws up her hands. "But we're just starting to have fun!"

"We'll play again later," Ram says. "I promise."

"I just wish you'd tell me what's so great about him," Daya grumbles. Ram wishes he could too. He'd love to show Daya the statues and the walls and the garden. He'd love someone else to see it.

But he can't. "Some other time." He starts to run.

"Wait," Daya shouts.

Ram pulls up. Daya rushes over, pushes the paper wrapper with the last two samosas at him. "Take them."

"Thanks! And we'll hit later. I swear it!"

When he gets back to the factory gate, a good

many of the workers are already making their way out and up the street.

He recognizes the faces of the other men who work the same shift as Nek. They mill out slowly, empty tiffins rattling at their sides as they walk or cycle away. He wonders how Nek has so much energy for working all day and then making statues at night.

"I've told you a dozen times!" Ram hears yelling from over the wall. "It is undignified!"

Then Ram hears a voice he recognizes. "But they are broken, sahib."

Ram edges around to peek. Nek stands with a man dressed in Western slacks and shirt. He wears a belt with a big round buckle. Both men have a hand on the bicycle that rests between them. The crate on the back sports an assortment of bicycle parts. Broken fenders, a gear missing half its teeth, part of a frame that was welded improperly. Ram understands immediately why Nek wants them. What he doesn't understand is why the foreman is so angry about it.

"Whether they are broken or not is beyond the matter. The matter is that they do not belong to you! Haven't I spoken to you about this before?"

"Yes, sir."

The man leans over the bicycle. "Do you know how many men come to our gates every day asking for work?"

Nek catches Ram staring. They both freeze for a second before Nek drops his eyes. "No, sir."

"You are lucky to have work at all! And no employee of the Hero Factory will leave looking like a lowly trash picker, is that clear?"

"But they are only going to be thrown out," Nek pleads.

The boss grows livid. "You will be thrown out!" he roars. "If we weren't so shorthanded with all those loafers off sick, I'd already have you out! This is your last warning. If I see so much as a single spoke in this basket of yours, you will no longer have a job. If you are collecting garbage, it means you are not working. And I will employ only men who work!"

Nek doesn't argue. Instead he wheels the bicycle over to a rubbish barrel and slowly—as if it hurts him to do so—begins to transfer the contents. The foreman and guard glower, hands on their hips. Nek takes his time, placing each piece carefully in the barrel so as not to make a sound. When he is done, he wheels the bicycle back around to face the two men.

"Last warning," the foreman says. "You are replaceable."

Nek keeps his eyes down. "Yes, sahib."

Without another word, the foreman stalks off. The guard turns away.

Ram feels he has seen something that he perhaps shouldn't have. Wishes for some reason he could unsee it. But he can't. He falls into step beside Nek, who has not yet mounted the bike.

They walk in silence past the shrine. At the corner, a bottle rocket explodes in the air above them. Ram glances back over his shoulder. Is Daya watching them now? But he doesn't see her.

Ram holds up the samosas. "Here."

Nek eyes them suspiciously.

"I didn't steal them," Ram says. "Honest, Uncle ji."

Now Nek laughs, only once, and not with conviction, but it is enough to banish the sting of the scene they have just left. "I am tired enough of my own cooking that I might have made an exception. *Chalo.*"

23

"Delicious," Nek announces as he finishes the last corner of his samosa. "Though not as good as the ones made by the man in my sector. He uses plenty of coriander—always fresh. Like my wife."

Ram's hands fall still, a section of glittering wire frozen between his finger and thumb. *Wife?* Nek is married? He is sure that Nek has never mentioned a wife before. "*You* are married?"

Nek nods, not even registering that he just told Ram something so shattering. But it is. Ram is shaken by the understanding that Nek is not as alone in the world as he himself is. And he wonders why it bothers him so much to learn this.

"Ayushee," he says. "We married four years ago."

Ram forces his hands to resume cutting the pieces. Still, he tells himself, Nek spends his days at work and his nights here in the garden. She must be mean, like Mrs. Singh. Nek hasn't even hinted at her existence in the whole month Ram has been working for him, so obviously he prefers Ram's company to that of his wife. This makes Ram feel a little better.

"You've never mentioned her before."

Nek considers, tilts his head. "Haven't I?"

"No."

"Huh," Nek says. "Maybe talking about her makes me miss her more. But I think about her all the time. It is like breathing. You don't tell yourself to breathe, but you keep going. She's with me like that. And the baby, of course."

Baby!? Ram fumbles a bangle and searches for it in the dirt at his feet.

"Why haven't you seen them in so long?" Ram manages to ask.

"The village I came from is nearly a whole day's journey by train. I cannot go more than once or twice a year."

"They should move to Chandigarh, then."

"We cannot afford it. I came here to work. It is cheaper for her to live there. I send most of my wages home. Someday when we save enough I can bring Ayushee and Vinod to the city."

Vinod. A boy's name. Nek has a son.

Ram wonders why it feels so much like a betrayal that the man already has a family hidden away. His fantasies about being secretly connected to Nek were ridiculous anyway. His daydreams about being someone special, like Rama, were just that— dreams. It is not Nek's fault Ram is alone, after all. Still, the bead at his chest feels like ice against his skin.

"Your job is important then," Ram says, recalling how the foreman at the factory scolded Nek. If he lost his job, he would not be able to send money to his family. If he lost his job, he would not be able to stay in Chandigarh at all. What would become of the garden then?

Nek sighs. "Yes. My job is important. But I don't like to be away. That is why I felt so lucky when I found your money. That windfall was almost enough to cover the ticket completely."

Ram feels awful. Awful that he gave Nek such a

terrible time about spending his money. Awful that when he learned Nek spent it on a train ticket, he was angry, jealous even. Now that he knows who Nek's going to see, he's ashamed of the anger. But he's also a tiny bit proud. After all, it was his money that made the visit possible.

"I wish I could go home more often. I miss them. More than Rama missed Sita even."

They work in silence for a few minutes, Ram making room in his mind for all he has just learned, packing up silly flights of thought and making space for what is true and real.

He remembers the chunk of the story Singh told him. "But I thought Sita and Lakshmana went along with Rama when he was exiled."

Nek skins the thinnest coating of concrete onto Sita's arm. "You heard that part already?"

"Yes." Ram scoots closer with the cut bangles.

"But not about how Lord Rama and Sita were separated?"

"Separated?" Ram asks. It doesn't make sense. Lord Rama was powerful. Lord Rama bent the bow of Shiva. And they were in love. . . . And Lakshmana was there to look after both of them too. "How?"

A grin plays at the corner of Nek's mouth. And

when the man speaks, his voice drops lower. "Not how," he says, "who."

A peacock shrieks in the distance. Ram jumps.

"Ravana."

For a while, Rama and Sita and Lakshmana lived happily in the jungle. They built a beautiful hut near a stream where they drew fresh water. They gathered fruits and nuts and hunted game and caught fish. They had adventures and climbed the hilltops by day, and sang and danced in the evenings. Sita charmed the beasts of the jungle, so that even the tigers would let her stroke their bellies like kittens.

But not all the creatures of the jungle were so gentle.

One day, a demoness called Surpanakha wandered

near where Rama was hunting. Instantly love-struck, she changed her form to that of a beautiful young woman and approached Rama.

"Marry me," she commanded. Surpanakha was not used to asking. Or being denied. So imagine her surprise when Rama laughed in her beautiful face.

"I am already wed to the loveliest woman in all the world."

The insulted Surpanakha began to transform, ready to pounce on the insulting man and rend him with her razor claws and sharp teeth. But Rama, perhaps out of pity, perhaps out of jest, said, "My brother Lakshmana is unmarried. And he is nearby. You might ask him."

Surpanakha hurried off to find Lakshmana. She found him pleasing enough, and commanded that he marry her as well. Lakshmana also refused. "How could I marry the likes of you when I know what true happiness is because of Rama and Sita?"

Surpanakha's disguise slipped, eyes growing buggy and red. "How dare you insult me?"

Lakshmana's hand twitched for his dagger. "I

mean no insult," he said carefully. "If you knew Sita, you would not take it is as such."

"Then I shall see this Sita for myself!" Surpanakha cried, growing into her true form. Yellow, warty skin. Stringy hair matted with the fur on her back. Rows of gray teeth dripped poison. "And we'll see how her beauty compares with mine when I've finished with her!"

Lakshmana knew now he was staring into the eyes of a *rakshasa*. He swung out with his sword. The demoness dodged the killing blow, but Lakshmana's blade sliced her nose cleanly off.

Surpanakha howled and fled. By now Rama had come running, drawn by the commotion. When he arrived, he found Lakshmana staring into the jungle, his sword dripping black blood.

"Should we pursue?" Lakshmana asked.

Rama shook his head. "Better to let her learn her lesson in peace. She will not bother us again."

But Rama was wrong.

Surpanakha rushed to *her* nearest brother, a demon called Khara. "I have been deeply insulted, brother! A pair of men in the jungle dishonored me, cut off my nose, and laughed at me!"

Khara didn't care much for his sister, but he dearly loved trouble. He assembled a small army of powerful demons and the next day marched out to attack Rama and Lakshmana.

The battle was as swift as it was brutal, but at the end, only Rama and Lakshmana remained. Surpanakha observed the defeat from afar, growing angrier and angrier as each demon fell to bow or sword.

However, she had more than one brother to ask for help.

Surpanakha flew south to Lanka, where her oldest brother, Ravana, had his kingdom. Ravana was the most powerful and evil of any *rakshasas* before or since. And he was clever. Early in his life, he tricked the gods into granting him a special gift: he could not be vanquished by any god in the heavens or any spirit from the underworld. So not only was he terrible, he was nearly immortal.

He was also enormous and strong, a muscled

torso from which sprouted twenty arms, all stout as tree trunks. Each arm could wield a powerful weapon. And on his shoulders rested ten heads, each with pointed teeth and wicked eyes.

Surpanakha filled all ten of Ravana's heads with lies about how poorly she'd been treated. She spun tales that Rama and Lakshmana had fallen upon Khara while he slept and slaughtered him without provocation. And for good measure, she claimed the princes had dared to insult mighty Ravana.

But it was Surpanakha's mention of the beautiful Sita that most piqued Ravana's interest. Like many a demon, Ravana had a great weakness for collecting pretty things. So if teaching these proud mortals a lesson meant adding another jewel to his collection, what could be the harm?

Together, Ravana and Surpanakha hatched a plan. Then, once they reached Rama's jungle, Surpanakha transformed herself into a beautiful golden doe and sprang into the clearing surrounding Rama and Sita's hut.

Sita was enchanted. "Rama!" she cried. "Please

catch that beautiful creature so that I might tame it as my pet!" Rama knew that Sita was often lonely when he and his brother went out hunting and seeking adventures, so he agreed. Still, something felt funny about the deer, and in his caution, Rama asked Lakshmana to keep careful guard over Sita.

Surpanakha bolted into the jungle, Rama chasing behind.

Ravana's plan was working. Within minutes, Rama's voice cried out in pain.

"Help me, brother!" came the anguished plea. "Oh, help!"

It wasn't Rama at all, of course. Surpanakha had led the great prince far away by now. But Ravana had dispatched another demon to mimic Rama's voice.

Sita's eyes grew wide. Rama was in trouble! And because he was chasing after something she had begged for like a spoiled child!

"Go, Lakshmana!"

But Lakshmana hesitated. "My brother has escaped countless dangers, with nary a scratch. This doesn't seem right."

The voice that was Rama's-not-Rama's screamed again, pleading for Lakshmana to come.

Sita was beside herself. "Please, Lakshmana!"

The voice sounded near enough, so Lakshmana fetched his sword. "Stay inside the hut," he ordered. Then he quickly cast a blessing of protection that the holy man had taught him long ago. The spell would prevent anyone from entering the hut.

Satisfied that Sita was safe, Lakshmana plunged into the jungle. That was when evil Ravana launched the final piece of his cunning plan. Taking the guise of a poor beggar, he hobbled into the clearing and fell to his knees just in front of the hut.

"Oh, most beautiful lady," Ravana cried pitifully. "I have wandered many days. I am weak with hunger. Please, give me something to eat?"

Sita could not let the poor man die, so she fetched food and water and rushed outside. As soon as she drew near, Ravana transformed himself and seized Sita about the waist.

She tried to wrestle free, furious with herself for forgetting Lakshmana's instructions.

First Ravana tried to woo Sita and flatter her so that she would come willingly. "Let me treat you as a queen should be treated. Not how this no-good prince of yours cares for you, in a hovel in the dark jungle."

"Never!" Sita raged defiantly.

Ravana didn't need her permission. He fetched Sita up and began flying with her back to Lanka. He would have her for his own one way or the other, and once she saw his palace, she would soften toward him, he was sure.

They sailed above the treetops. As they flew, a brave vulture called Jatayu saw them, recognized Sita, and swooped at Ravana, hoping to help the princess. With one of his twenty arms, Ravana drew a sword, sliced Jatayu's wing off with a single stroke, and sent the noble bird plummeting back to earth. Swiftly, Ravana raced homeward with his prize.

What happened then?" Ram asks, his mind awhirl with shape-shifting demons, a captured princess, and plummeting birds. "Did Rama catch him?" Ram nestles another of the bangle fragments into place. Sita's sleeve is only half-done, but already she shimmers.

"When I get back," Nek says. "I need to prepare for my journey."

"How long will you be gone again?"

"The village is only a few hundred kilometers away, but the journey is slow. There is only one daily train there and back. It takes the better part of the day to get home. I have one day with my family, and then I return to be back for work on Tuesday. Three days."

All that trouble and expense for only a single day with his family? No wonder Nek can't make the journey more often.

Still, three days sounds like forever. And with the holiday, even Daya won't be around as much as usual. At least Ram has Sita.

"You are sure you know what to do? You know how thick to make the mortar? How to place the pieces?" Nek worries.

"I won't let you down," Ram says.

Nek seems exhausted. A light sweat beads on his brow, though the air is chilly.

"Are you all right, Uncle ji?" Ram asks.

Nek blinks. "Just tired. Some of the men at the factory have been out sick. The boss has made me do some extra sweeping."

Ram remembers how the boss yelled at Nek. He was mean. Like one of the pesky demons from the story. Nek is working too hard.

"You really should go to school, Ram," he says. But he doesn't say it like he believes it will happen, only that he wishes it would.

"School isn't for me," Ram says, mixing up more cement.

"Yes, it is," Nek said. "You're too smart not to go to school."

"I don't even know how to read."

"That kind of smart they can teach. You have all the other kinds they can't."

Nek's praise surprises Ram. Nek quickly adds, "But even Rama had a teacher. Even Rama had things he couldn't learn on his own. Do you think you're better than him?"

"No, Uncle ji." If Nek thinks Ram can do it, maybe he could. Maybe school wouldn't be the worst thing. He'd like to prove Nek right, he thinks. Pass another true test.

"I will make sure Vinod goes to a proper school," Nek says as he digs into his pocket. He pulls two coins out and extends them to Ram. "Your pay. I won't be here tomorrow."

Ram hesitates. "You need it. For your journey."

"*Nahi*," Nek says. "I have enough."

Ram closes his hand around the coins. "*Shukriya*."

Nek places a hand on Ram's shoulder, pats it once, and walks away. "You're not so bad, Ram." For some reason, Ram cannot reply.

Ram is back at first light the next day. He works all day cutting bangles, placing them just so.

He realizes by lunchtime that if he keeps working like this, he'll finish Sita before Nek gets back. And suddenly that's all he wants to do, to finish off the statue and surprise Nek. So he does, taking breaks only to duck out and grab food, dragging himself back to his rooftop to sleep at night.

Late on the second afternoon, his belly all at once screams at him to fill it. He's been so focused on Sita that he forgot to stop for lunch.

She is closer. The mosaic of bangles and wire

is the most beautiful thing Ram has ever seen. He can't believe he had any part of it.

"I'll be right back," he says, and he realizes with a start that now even he is talking to the statues. But he doesn't care. It puts him in good company.

He heads back to the sector to see if Rakesh has anything left over. But when he gets there, he notices the shrine is overflowing. Ram nabs a stack of parathas, a little silk bag tied up with string, and an apple without breaking stride.

On the walk back he shoves one paratha whole into his mouth and starts working on the string. Inside the bag are roasted cashews. Cashews! Ram hasn't had cashews in ages. He tosses one into his mouth, the salt and sweet crunching together.

The apple is nearly gone when he reaches the edge of the sector and the new road. Ram gnaws the core with his front teeth, sucking the last precious drops of juice. He chucks the core over his shoulder and starts across the unbuilt road to the forest. But then Ram freezes.

Six or seven boys stand at the edge of the trees, blocking the path. They are back. And they have seen him, he can tell. But he ducks down and crouches behind the dirt pile anyway.

They are waiting for him.

He'll have to run again.

But they've chased him close twice now.

If they keep chasing him . . . If he keeps running . . .

The garden. They know where to find him. If they know where to find him, they'll eventually know what's inside the jungle.

He won't let that happen.

He knows what he must do.

Ram climbs over the dirt and into the road. A few of the boys step forward. He pulls his bundle from his pocket. Nek has paid him some. There is what he earned running errands for Singh and hitting *gilli*. And he's saved most of it, eating from the shrine or getting food from Daya.

The broken watch is another matter, but he slips it off his wrist anyway.

Ram walks over to them. His heart pounds in his ears and his breathing is too quick.

"Fine, you win," Ram says, tipping all his money into his palm along with the watch. "Take it." He hopes the boys don't realize that he is only pretending to be brave. He hopes they don't notice how his hand trembles as he offers the money. A thought flits through his head: Had Rama pretended too when he faced demons? Maybe he felt just as scared as Ram does now.

When the pack sees he will not run, they regroup into a solid clump, like one body with many heads and arms. Like Ravana himself.

"Why aren't you running this time, rat?" Peach Fuzz asks. He seems not so big out of his school jacket and tie, but still big enough.

Ram swallows hard, tries to sound confident, like he imagines Rama would have. "I get tired of running."

Peach Fuzz wears a wicked smile. "Tired? I didn't know *dogs* got tired."

Behind them in the city, the fireworks have begun. Ram can hear their distant shrieks, the boom rolling over them a second later.

All he wants them to do is go away. To leave him and the garden alone. He thrusts his hand forward. "Take it and go."

Peach Fuzz squints, steps closer, and pokes Ram in the spot where his collar opens up. His fingernail is long enough and he presses hard enough that Ram is sure he'll have a little crescent-shaped line on his chest. He takes the money with his other hand, shoves it in his pocket. Then he snatches the watch. *Maybe he won't notice it's broken,* Ram hopes. *Maybe—*

But Peach Fuzz holds it up to catch the street light. "You broke it!" He sounds horrified.

"It was an accident—"

"My father is going to kill me," Peach Fuzz says, forgetting to sound tough for a moment.

"You have what you came for," Ram says. "Now go."

Peach Fuzz's toughness comes back. "No! Now you owe us for the watch, too!" His breath stinks of onions as he leans close.

"It's all I have!"

"Plus, you cheated us. You have to pay for that, too."

It takes every drop of self-control Ram can muster not to spit back that he won the money fair and square. That if they were half as good at *gilli* as they thought they were, it wouldn't have been so easy to win against them.

If Rama and Lakshmana were dealing with these bullies, they'd slice off a few ears or noses or scare them with one twang of a bowstring. But he's not Rama. And he's alone.

"But I have no more."

"Triple what you stole."

None of this is going the way it was supposed to. If he weren't so worried for the garden, he'd be furious. "You're *pagal* if—"

Peach Fuzz's fist lands solidly in Ram's stomach. He doubles over, gasps, but then a popping sound like fireworks explodes against his temple.

Ram drops.

Peach Fuzz stoops over. "Look at me, dog."

Ram can only open one eye. The boys are all knotted together. Arms and legs. Shadows and malice. "We know what you're hiding. We've found all that junk in there, those weird statues." Ram feels something like a stone land on his chest. He knows what it is, and his heart sinks. "Bring the money here. The day after Diwali. If you don't, we'll figure out who you stole those statues from. Whose land you're squatting on in that jungle. And I know very important people in the city who can come and knock it all down with great bulldozers. And after they knock it all down, they'll send you to jail, or wherever trash like you ends up."

Ram closes a fist around the object on his chest. Shiva's eye.

The day after Diwali. Two days from now.

The boys walk away. When their footsteps have faded completely, Ram manages to stand. He staggers into the shadows of the garden.

He needs to figure out what to do. But he's so tired. And his head hurts.

Ram collapses at Sita's feet, and then rolls over, knees poking up in the air. Two days. He doesn't even know how much triple the money would be. Not that it matters. There is no way he can get it.

And Nek. What will Nek say? He forgave him once, but will he again?

He hears a twig snap on the path and sits up so fast his brain seems to bounce against the inside of his skull.

"Ram?" Daya whispers from the shadows.

Ram's mouth feels full of cotton. It hurts to talk. "What are you doing here, Daya?"

Daya rushes into the clearing. "Vijay . . . he . . . he hit you!"

"I was there, Daya," Ram says. "I know."

Ram must look awful for Daya to be so worried. "Your lip is bleeding!"

"Did they see you?"

"I followed you. I saw you get something from the shrine and I was mad at you, so I followed you, again. Ram! I warned you about them, didn't I?"

"But did they see you?"

She shakes her head. "I hid at the corner, but I heard what they said, Ram. What is happening?"

Ram touches his eye. "You crossed the road."

"I had to see if you were hurt! We have to go to Papa!"

Ram seizes her arm. "No!"

Daya shakes loose. "He will help you, Ram. Whatever it is you're protecting here—" She stops, her expression softening. "Oh."

Ram knows she is seeing Sita. And despite the pain, despite all the trouble, despite how complicated everything is becoming, he finds himself pleased at her reaction.

"Oh, Ram," Daya says. "Did you make this?"

"With my friend, Nek uncle."

Daya crouches in front of the statue. The light is dusky now, and Sita is less glorious than when the sun dappled through the leaves and shimmered against the bangles. But she dazzles, still. "*Hoye, hoye*," Daya whispers.

"I still have to finish. She'll be covered all over when I'm done."

"She's so pretty already. Papa will be so proud."

The thought tempts Ram. He shoves it aside. "No one can know." And he tells her why. He tells her about Nek. About what he makes here, how he does it, how Ram came to help him. And that if the secret is known, then Nek will get into trouble. The whole place could disappear.

Daya is quiet. "There are more of these statues?"

"Hundreds," Ram says. The volume of what Nek has made feels like a burden to him now. So many. All of them in danger.

"I want to see them. Papa will want to see them. He can help, Ram," Daya says urgently.

"I promised Nek uncle to keep it secret. He's away until the morning after tomorrow. Maybe then I can talk to him. We can figure out what to do. But I have to come up with the money—"

"Papa has money!" Daya pleads. Ram knows Singh would likely share. But he'd also demand to know what the money was for. And how can he explain? Without betraying Nek?

"And he knows people at the city! Lots who might—"

"No," Ram decides. "Not yet. Not until I talk to Nek uncle."

Daya deflates.

"Promise me, Daya." Ram is grasping her arm. "Promise you won't tell him."

Daya gazes at Sita. "You're wrong," she says. "But *theek hai*."

Ram struggles to his feet. The pain in his head is ebbing, and he has his breath back. He holds out his hand. "Come on. I'll walk you back."

Daya stands. "Show me the animals first."

Ram grins. She's already seen this much. And she's promised to keep the secret. He supposes she deserves something.

"*Chalo*," he says. "But we have to get you back before sundown."

If Daya is as scared of snakes or other things as Ram had been when he first visited the garden, she doesn't show it. "This place is wonderful!"

Ram figures she's brave because he's with her. The trees feel friendlier, the shadows mysterious instead of threatening. He tells her proudly about all the *real* animals he's seen here—the pangolin and the birds and the mongoose he heard once. He points out one of the gooseberry trees and pulls tiny twigs from a neem tree for them to chew as they walk.

When they reach the menagerie, and Daya is short enough that she doesn't have to duck under the arched doorways. He shows her the laughing army, and the someday waterfall, and Shiva up on top. The only thing he doesn't show her is the village. He figures that is Nek's alone to share.

Daya's wonder grows at every new corner. When they get back to Sita, Ram shows her how he's been building the pattern.

Daya sighs, her breath spiced by the bitter twigs they've been chewing. "Poor Sita. Kidnapped. Why do girls in the stories never get to do anything good besides get rescued?"

"So Rama and Lakshmana do rescue her?" Ram asks. He figured as much. Why else have all these festivals and parades if the story ended unhappily?

"Eventually," Daya snorts. "But only because she's so smart. And even then they take forever."

"Why forever?" And Ram realizes as he says it, as Daya looks at him with wonder, that he's forgotten to pretend that he already knows it all. But he doesn't care. "What happens next, Daya?"

Rama chased the golden deer that was Surpanakha for hours. Since Sita had begged him to capture it for a pet, he had to stalk quietly. Every time he drew near enough to pounce, wily Surpanakha sprinted away, leading Rama farther and farther afield. When they were half a day's journey gone, Surpanakha resumed her form, slunk into the treetops, and flew away. She would not dare face Rama alone, not after the way he and Lakshmana had humiliated her first brother's army. Besides, her ends had been met. Sita was ripped from the prince, and now Rama would suffer for having rejected Surpanakha.

Rama realized the deer's trail had vanished. And then he began to wonder how the animal had been able to evade him for so long. Worry puffed up inside him like bread baking in the tandoor. He raced home.

Meanwhile, Lakshmana chased the anguished cries of Rama in the opposite direction. The demon threw his voice all around the jungle, confusing Lakshmana. But Lakshmana would not abandon his brother and followed the voice all the way to the mountains on the eastern edge of the forest. Coming into the foothills, the demon gave a final cackle in his very own voice, and Lakshmana knew at once that he had been duped. If he had been tricked, perhaps Rama had as well!

He hurried back, exploding into the clearing at the same time as Rama.

"We've been deceived!" Rama said to his brother. "Is Sita safe?"

The hut was empty.

"Sita!" Rama called. "Where are you?"

In the distance, they heard a bird's call. But not just any bird's call. The squawking croak of a vulture repeating Rama's name, over and over, like a prayer.

"I've already followed one foolish voice today," Lakshmana told his brother. "I don't know if—"

But Rama was already gone.

Lakshmana, like always, followed. Soon they found poor Jatayu, the vulture who had tried to slow Ravana down as he fled with Sita.

The noble bird, his great wing divided from his body, had but moments left to live. "A demon king," Jatayu said, "such as I have never seen. With many heads, even more arms . . . He has taken your Sita."

"Where?" Rama asked, panicked.

Jatayu's words came weaker than before. "South," he breathed as his soul slipped loose, and he fell silent.

"Lakshmana," Rama said, "come quickly."

Lakshmana held up a hand. "Jatayu gave his life to help us. We must show him honor before we go."

As anxious as he was to search for Sita, Rama knew his brother was right. Together they thanked the bird for his sacrifice, prayed for his soul to find peace.

When they finished, Lakshmana stood. "Now we will find Sita."

They ran south. As they went, Rama called up to the birds in the treetops, asking if any had seen a great demon clutching the beautiful Sita. None had.

Just as they began to lose hope, Lakshmana caught a glimpse of something gold glittering from a branch high overhead. "There, Rama!"

Rama climbed the tree hastily, and then jumped back down. In his palm was a thin gold bangle, set with a tiny ruby. "This is Sita's!"

"It must have fallen from her as she struggled!"

"Or maybe she dropped it on purpose, for us to follow," Lakshmana suggested.

Indeed she had. A few miles farther, they found a ring. Clever Sita had left a glittering trail for the brothers to follow. And she had plenty of jewels to throw, marking out a path. Confident now of their direction, the brothers ran.

29

The light is almost completely gone when Daya finishes the story. Ram walks her back to 22, where her father will be waiting. Daya is uncharacteristically quiet.

When they reach the corner, Ram hangs back. "Aren't you coming?" Daya asks.

"I can't. See you tomorrow, though?"

"Tomorrow is Diwali," Daya says. "I'll be at home all day. Everybody will."

"Oh, right."

"What are you going to do, Ram?" Daya asks. Now that she has seen the garden, now that she knows what is at stake, she seems to understand the hugeness of the problem, the complications of asking for help when all that help will come at a price.

"Nek uncle will know what to do," Ram says. "I will wait for him at the factory when he is due back. Maybe we will come to your father together. Do you really think he will help?"

Daya brightens. "I know he will, Ram. He likes you. And he'll like anybody who can make such wonderful things. He will figure out a way."

"I hope you are right. But promise not to say anything? Until I speak to Nek uncle?"

Daya nods. "Promise."

Ram takes a few steps back. "Happy Diwali, then."

Daya hesitates, then runs over and throws her arms around Ram's neck. She squeezes hard, and then runs away without another word.

Ram walks back, thinking. Rama and Lakshmana didn't know what to do when Sita was taken, any more than Ram knows what to do now. But they had faith. They found the bracelet, and then they found her ring. They kept going.

And Ram knows that this is what he must do. He has no idea how this all will end, only what he must do next.

❧❧❧

Ram works late into the night, burning tire after tire, the oily smoke clinging to his hair and clothes. When he finally drags himself under his sign to get a little sleep, he knows the clock has rounded the bend to the next day already. It is Diwali. The lamps in the windows of the apartments burn, and the peace of the city at night seems out of touch with the turmoil Ram feels inside.

Still, he is so, so tired.

The next day is a cold one. Ram huddles under his blanket. The street below is eerily quiet.

The holiday. Of course. No workers at the factory.

But he still has work to do. So he hurries to the garden.

Sita's dress is nearly done. But that last bit will take the longest, the fold up and over her shoulder.

He can do it.

He works, mixing mortar, placing pieces, gradually sweeping the pattern up and over the shoulder of the statue. He stops now and then to cut more bangles, worrying he won't have enough. But when he at last manages to finish the pattern, he has a few pieces to spare.

Good. Nek will be pleased. But something is

off now. The sari looks like it's been placed on a department store mannequin. As if the sari is the point. And it isn't, Ram realizes. It is only part of it.

Her features will matter. Yes, of course, the eyes and a mouth. And her head is too bald. The soldiers and Lakshmana all wore puzzled together pot fragments for helmets. But a helmet for Sita? No. What would Nek have been imagining?

Then he considers the silky *dupatta*, the little round mirrors. "You might be right," he says to the statue.

He fetches it from the supply tarp. The mortar is still too wet around Sita's shoulders for him to try it now, but he holds it up and away, a little behind the forehead, like a veil.

Yes.

If he cuts out the mirrored part and uses that only, it will be just the right size. He can attach it with a skim coat of mortar, but not until the pieces of bangle on Sita's shoulders and back dry. Not until tomorrow.

When Nek returns.

It will be enough time to finish her.

It will have to be.

How can time fly and creep at once? Maybe it is like the dark magic out of the Rama stories. Maybe it is the kind of torment Ravana and his demons might have plagued people with. All the horrible desperation of hurrying combined with all the torture of waiting, without the anticipation of waiting for anything good.

So both finally and too quickly, Diwali comes and goes. The last two days have been the longest and shortest Ram has ever known, but finally they end.

Ram waits outside the gates the next morning as the factory reopens. If he can catch Nek before work, it will be better than trying to explain it all at lunch, when they'll need to go see Singh.

The plan has been building in his mind since Daya left him. It will work.

It will have to.

But first he must speak to Nek.

The workers straggle in, Ram recognizing a few from Nek's shift.

But when the guard swings the gate shut, Nek has not appeared. Has Ram missed him?

Nek's bicycle—his unmistakable one with the rusted fender and the giant crate tied onto the rear rack—is not underneath the tree where he parks it every day.

"You!" The guard has seen him now. The man is gangly, face scarred by deep pits up and down the hollows of his cheeks. "Shoo!"

"Where is Nekji?" Ram asks, backing up a step so the guard can't grab him if he is of a mind to.

"Go beg somewhere else!" The guard's military-style cap is fraying at the edges, one thread hanging down his forehead.

"Nek!" Ram repeats, standing his ground. "Why isn't his bicycle by the tree?"

The guard stops. "The trashman?" He is almost

smiling as he says it. But it is not a friendly smile. "The one who tries to steal the rubbish to take home with him?"

Ram wants to shout that he doesn't take it home. He takes it somewhere better, makes it into something better. But this man wouldn't understand. And it wouldn't help.

The guard waves a hand at Ram. "Not here. Probably not ever again. The boss was already mad at him for stealing trash. He won't take the idiot back after he decided to shirk on a day when we're shorthanded."

Won't take him back? But Nek needs this job. His family relies on the money. Ram knows that he would not simply skip work.

Something is wrong. Maybe his train was delayed? Or he extended his visit a little longer?

Ram's mind whirls. Or would he just stay altogether? Abandon the garden? Abandon Ram?

No. Not Nek.

Ram runs in the direction of Mani Marg, the street Nek has mentioned once or twice.

31

Ram knows Mani Marg well enough but wishes he'd thought earlier to ask Nek where his house was. Mani Marg is a smaller street than his own, in a quieter sector. He runs past the market and shops in the center, dodges a grocer with a broom who figures he has come to steal. He stands on the corner of the street, watches the rickshaw and cycles and trucks swirl around the roundabout, and tries to focus. How will he find Nek?

He walks from one end to the other, back and forth, over and over, hoping for something, anything that will point him in the right direction.

There is a multistory apartment house—maybe eight levels high—all concrete and right angles and tiny windows. Could Nek live in one of those rooms? Then there are windows open in the upstairs above some of the shops, and once in a while he sees a woman shaking out a rug or resting her chin in her hand.

Please, he thinks, *please let me find him!*

He tries asking shopkeepers. Most of them shoo him away as soon as they see him approaching. And when he catches sight of himself in the polished window of a fabric seller, he can guess why.

His hair is filthy. What isn't slicked down by sweat is matted and stands up defiantly. His one eye is twice the size of the other, what with the swelling from the beating he took. Not to mention his bare feet, black and dusty, his raggedy pants and tunic.

He does his best to tidy the hair, licks a finger and scrubs at his face the best he can, but it is hopeless. Besides, the few shopkeepers who aren't immediately appalled at his appearance are no more helpful. They know no man named Nek who works at the factory in Sector 22.

Ram leans against a tree. What can he do now? What could he ever do? Filthy and bruised, exhausted and hungry. The smell of the samosas from the stand across the street makes it hard to concentrate—

Samosas!

Ram plunges into the street, dodging carts and cycles and pedestrians. The samosa seller is helping a young woman when Ram draws near the bright umbrella shading his operation. He can smell the rich potatoes and lamb, the heaviness of the hot oil lingering like a rain cloud. A great mound of coriander spices the air.

He bounces on his toes while he waits for the woman to finish her purchase. Then the vendor turns to him. He is ready to be polite, but Ram sees the transformation as the man recognizes Ram as a beggar or thief or worse.

"Go!"

"Please!" Ram begs, sure that this is the place. Sure this must be the man whose samosas Nek praised. "I do not wish to trouble you, Uncle. But do you know a man called Nekji?"

"I have customers to tend to," the man says automatically, though no one is waiting for him.

"Nekji," Ram repeats. "He works at the factory in Twenty-Two. He rides a bicycle with a great basket attached to the back. Do you know him?"

The man attacks the pile of coriander with a stubby knife, muttering.

Ram's shoulders slump, his heart caving in on itself. It was a dumb idea. But it was his only one.

The sound of chopping stops suddenly. "Did you say Nekji?"

Ram whips around.

The man points with the knife to an alley. "Down there. But I haven't seen him in a few days—"

Ram doesn't wait for him to finish.

He races down the alley, into the shadows. There are different smells here that make him miss the samosa stand immediately, ones strong enough to make him lose his appetite. A few doors line the sides, but there is nothing written on them, no names or addresses to confirm that someone lives inside them.

And then Ram sees it at the end of the alley.

Chained up and locked to the railing of a stairway that looks as if it might collapse at any moment is Nek's bicycle. At the top of the stair is a flat wooden door, green enamel peeling in great strips. A small window next to it stands open, the curtain drawn. "Hello?"

When there is no answer, Ram puts his foot on the first step.

"Uncle ji?"

He keeps climbing, the stairs shifting and wobbling as he goes higher.

At the top, he knocks softly at the door. "Uncle ji?" he repeats. "It's Ram."

He waits, listens. Nothing. The window is not positioned over the landing, but if he climbs out on the railing, he might be able to peek in. He has always been a good climber.

The stairs lurch in warning as he hops onto the rail. Ram freezes, squatting like a monkey on a wire, waiting just a beat to see if the rail will support him. When it doesn't seem to want to move any more, he creeps his feet closer to the edge, straightening his legs as he slowly stands to reach for the window.

The room is dark and small and close, with a pallet in one corner and a small table and two chairs in another. A door on the opposite side is shut tight, leading perhaps to a bathroom or a hall, Ram guesses.

The room seems empty.

But then the pallet shifts, and the blanket on top reveals a hand in the shadows.

"Uncle ji?" Ram whispers.

"Who's there?" Nek's voice is weak, but unmistakably his. Ram doesn't wait for more. He heaves himself over the sill and tumbles through the window.

Ram crashes onto the tile floor. A sour smell soaks the room.

"Who's there?" Nek repeats.

Ram jumps up, hurries over to the pallet. "Uncle ji?"

It is so dark in the room. There is a lamp fixed to the ceiling, but he cannot find a switch. An oil lamp sits on the little table. Ram finds a match, lights it, and carries it over.

Nek's eyes are sunken, his forehead glistens in the lamplight. He squints against the light as it draws closer.

"Ram?" Nek moves to sit up, but falls back against the ticking.

The foul smell is stronger here. Ram spies a bucket by the bedside. He moves it carefully as he holds his breath. He can feel the heat rising off Nek even from a distance, and even though the man has himself buried in blankets.

"My garden," Nek sounds as if he is remembering. "Ram."

"You are sick."

"I was sick on the train. I hope Ayushee and Vinod are all right. They were fine when I left them."

Ram remembers how tired Nek was the night before he left. He was sick even before he left, Ram figures.

He wonders what to do now. His whole plan hinged on introducing Nek and Singh, seeing what Singh could do to help, maybe getting him to buy a statue for the museum. Surely Nek would let *one* statue go if it meant possibly saving the rest of the garden.

But Nek is in no shape to do anything. And he has no one to help him. No one but Ram.

What to do?

"Is there water?" Nek asks.

An empty glass sits on the floor beside the pallet. Ram snatches it up. A small cupboard on the wall under the window serves as the kitchen. A great clay jug with a spigot sits on the side of the little sink, which is really just an enamel bowl. There are no pipes for the water to drain out.

Ram fills the glass, sloshing the water over the top as he carries it back to Nek. He holds the rim to the man's mouth, helps him drink. Even lifting his head from the pillow seems to exhaust Nek.

"I must go to work." Nek's voice is garbled, as if the water is sticking in his throat. He is in no state to stand, much less work. Besides, Ram knows Nek may have no job to go to.

"You must rest."

Nek's eyes flash doubt. "*Nahi*. The boss—"

"You are sick. You should eat."

Ram doesn't know the first thing about caring for a sick person, as he's never been cared for himself. But he knows that eating is usually a good idea. He scans the little shelves under the basin. Dried lentils, rice, an onion, a few jars of spices Ram can't read the labels of. Two small cooking pots and a frying pan occupy the bottom shelf. The little stove is really just a burner sitting on the tabletop, attached to a can of propane.

Ram knows even less about cooking than he does

about taking care of the sick. But he knows about getting food.

His hand goes to his money pouch, but then he remembers he gave all his coins to the gang.

"I'm going to get you some food," Ram says. "I'll be right back."

Nek doesn't answer, but he rolls to one elbow and gestures at the table. A small tin sits in the middle. Coins rattle in the bottom as Ram pries the lid off. He picks a few rumpled paper notes, finds a pair of keys hung on a wire ring buried under them. One is larger, silver and flat. The key to the door, Ram guesses. The smaller one must belong to the padlock on the bicycle. He tucks the keys into his pocket along with the money.

"Do you . . ." Ram doesn't know how to ask the question without embarrassing Nek. "Is there a toilet here?"

Nek points at the door opposite the entrance. "Down the hall. Shared."

Ram takes a breath, picks up the foul-smelling bucket with his fingertips, and carries it down the dark hall to a small bathroom. He empties the pail into the hole in the floor, opens the taps, and rinses the bucket out the best he can.

Nek hasn't moved by the time Ram returns. "Do you need—" Ram jerks his head back to the bathroom. The man shakes his head.

Ram replaces the pail. "I'll be back soon."

This time he uses the door, locking it behind him with the key, and flies down the stairs to find food.

33

Ram fumbles with the key in the lock when he returns, worried that he's taken too long. He managed to pick up some apples from a shrine at the corner, a little packet of cooked rice and dal and boiled potato from the man at the samosa stand. He also saw the green cross on the white-painted sign hanging above a shop. It took plenty of waving around of the money he'd brought from Nek's tin to convince the chemist that he hadn't come to steal or beg. Once it was clear he was a paying customer, the chemist sold him a small packet of chalky pills that he said would do for fever. Ram hopes he is right.

Inside, he sets the bundle on the little table and pulls a spoon from a teacup beneath the basin.

"Uncle ji?" Ram asks as he kneels by the bed with the food balanced on one palm. He checks the pail. Still empty. A good sign, he hopes.

Nek's eyes flutter open.

"I brought food." Ram dips the spoon into the packet, tilts it into Nek's mouth. Nek chews forever, Ram worrying that maybe feeding him isn't the right thing to do.

He jumps up, grabs the paper envelope containing the pills, and tips two into his palm. "Here!" He holds them out to Nek. "Take these. For your fever."

Nek accepts the pills, swallows them with a gulp of water.

"Thank you."

Encouraged, Ram picks up the rice again. Nek takes half a dozen bites more before he indicates that he is done. In moments he is asleep again.

Ram sits back against the wall. Hungry, he eats half the mixture before he remembers he ought to save some for when Nek wakes. He wraps the rest back in the waxy paper, and then bites into one of the apples. He's shocked at the noise, but Nek does not stir. Ram munches away, walking around the little room. A small chest sits on the wall opposite where Nek sleeps. Inside are a couple of changes of clothing, an extra blanket. Ram takes the blanket and lays it at the end of the bed in case Nek needs it later. On a shelf above the chest is a cup, a toothbrush, a razor, and a cake of soap. Above the shelf hangs a mirror, cloudy with age. Pasted to the corner of the mirror is a photograph. Ram leans close.

The photo is black and white, but the image clear. A young woman sits in a stiff wooden chair against a plain background. She is lovely, though she looks serious or afraid, as if she isn't sure about having her picture taken. A thick black braid drapes over one shoulder. Her clothing is simple, but Ram notices a fine border of embroidery at the edge of her *dupatta* and at the cuffs of her *salwar* suit.

In her lap, a baby sleeps, eyes shut tight, fists curled.

Ayushee and Vinod.

Ram stares a little longer. The woman in the photo has no idea Nek is in trouble. Only Ram knows. Only Ram can help.

He is beginning to understand how. He will still talk to Singh. But without Nek. It will be a gamble.

But he has no other choice. And he has preparations to make, a few details to finish. . . .

But not until Nek improves.

Ram waits. An hour, maybe more, before Nek stirs.

"What happened to your face?" Nek asks. The man's eyes seem more alert. Maybe the pills are helping.

"Do you want food? Water?" Ram asks, rising from the wooden chair he's been camped in.

"What happened to you?"

It feels like weeks ago that he let the gang of boys catch him, though it was only the day before yesterday. "Nothing."

"How did your eye get so swollen?"

"I . . ." Ram nervously rubs the bead between his fingers. "When I came through the window, I hit my head on the corner of the cupboard."

Nek considers the lie, but lets it pass. Then he smiles. "When you clambered through that window, I could only see your silhouette. I thought you were a monkey come to snatch food."

Ram grins. "I'm bigger than a monkey," he says. "But I climb almost as well."

Nek's eyes fall shut again, and Ram wonders if

he has passed back into sleep. But then he speaks. "And you came to help me."

"I was worried," Ram explains. "When you did not come to the garden. And when I could not find you at the factory. I wanted to help."

"We all need help sometimes, don't we?" Nek says. His eyes are brighter, but still sunk deep in his face. His voice is still quiet, but not as wispy as before. He looks better, Ram decides. Not well, but better. "Have I told you yet how Hanuman helped Rama?"

Ram hesitates. Of course he wants to hear the story. But Nek should rest. And Ram has other work still to do. But he can spare a few minutes. And if Nek can get through the tale, it will be a good indication that he will be strong enough for Ram to leave him on his own. Ram sits, tucks his feet behind the braces of the wooden chair.

"Who was Hanuman?"

34

Rama and Lakshmana collected bangles, earrings, anklets, and even precious stones that Sita flicked free of her rings and necklaces. But after months of pursuit, over hill and mountain, the trail grew cold. Days passed without finding so much as a speck of gold. Rama and Lakshmana began to lose heart. But as they searched and their spirits grew lower, *someone* found them.

In the shadow of Mount Rishyamukha, there dwelled a band of monkeys. These monkeys were extraordinary, of the kind that no longer exists in India. They were closer to men in their thoughts and statures, but with the long tails and kind faces of the lesser monkeys. This band of monkeys was exiled. Their king, Sugriva, had been overthrown by his wicked brother, Vali. Vali had taken Sugriva's wife and his throne, and the usurped king had taken refuge in the forest with a handful of his loyal followers.

Among these followers was a monkey named Hanuman.

Hanuman's story was as full of magic as Rama's. From the time he was small, he'd been a great favorite of Vishnu, who had blessed Hanuman with great gifts and abilities.

He had protection from danger, a great power to leap so that it seemed as if he could fly, and the ability to change his shape and size at will. When he saw Rama and Lakshmana in the forest, he felt drawn to them, sensing that perhaps it was *dharma* that they meet.

Hanuman approached the brothers, offering food and shelter if they would accompany him back to meet the king of the monkeys. Tired and hungry from their long search, the brothers gladly followed.

When they arrived at Sugriva's camp, they were surprised to find the king in such humble circumstances, living among the treetops rather than in his palace.

King Sugriva wrung his tail, ashamed, as he explained his exile.

"Then you must steal your kingdom and your bride back," Lakshmana said.

"I wish it were so simple. My brother, Vali, is too powerful. When anyone gets near enough to fight him in battle, he can steal half their strength and wield it as his own."

"Then attack him from a distance," Lakshmana said.

Again, the monkey king said no. "We have tried. But my brother can also thicken his hide, so that it is like the trunks of seven trees. No arrow can pierce such armor."

Rama was moved. How similar his own circumstances were to Sugriva's. Like Rama, Sugriva's love had been taken from him. Like Rama, he had been exiled from his rightful home. "I will help you."

Hanuman's heart leaped inside him. This Rama truly

was noble if he was willing to help Sugriva and face a terrible enemy when he had no part in the conflict.

"What can you do?" Sugriva asked. "Not even Hanuman can defeat him, though he alone of my great warriors survived our last battle with Vali."

Rama did not like to boast. "My brother is able," Lakshmana said in his stead.

With nothing to lose, Sugriva followed them as they marched to his former kingdom. He was over-joyed when Rama and Lakshmana made short work of the usurping Vali.

Reunited with his wife and restored to his throne, Sugriva presented Rama with a priceless gift: a col-lection of precious stones, gold, and silver that he and his followers had found while in exile.

Rama's eyes grew wide. They were Sita's jewels!

"Where did you find these?" he asked eagerly.

"In the forest where we camped," Hanuman explained.

"Scattered about?"

Hanuman considered. "In a sort of line, leading south."

"Sita's trail!" Rama exclaimed. "Show us where you found the last jewel."

"My whole army will march with you," Sugriva said.

"No," Rama said. "Not yet. When we need your help, we will send for you."

"Then take Hanuman," Sugriva urged. "He found the jewels. And he can fetch us when you require aid."

Hanuman was thrilled. He led Rama and Lakshmana to where he'd found the last of Sita's gems. They searched on and found another, and then another. Soon they came to the southern shore. And sure enough, they found one last bloodred ruby on the sand.

On the far horizon, a great green island rose out of the sea.

"What is that place?" Rama asked.

"Lanka," Hanuman said. "The island stronghold of Ravana and his *rakshasa* army."

Ravana, thought Rama. "Does this Ravana have many heads and arms?"

"Ten heads," Hanuman said. "And twenty arms. And an appetite for trouble that is even greater."

Rama didn't care. He only cared that he was now so near to Sita and the end of his quest. "We must find a boat."

"Wait, Rama," Hanuman said. "I can cross over."

"You?"

Hanuman had kept his gifts secret until now. But he knew that if the gods had had a reason for blessing him with such powers, this must be it.

"Please stand back."

Rama and Lakshmana stepped back from Hanuman. And to their shock, the monkey began to grow. Where before he only reached their shoulders, he soon grew as tall as the great banyan tree where the holy man had led them so long ago.

"Wonderful!" Rama said. "But now what?"

"Now, I jump." Hanuman grinned. "I'll find Sita and then come back to you."

Hanuman vaulted over the ocean and landed on Lanka, only a tiny puff of sand rising up around his feet. He shrank back to his normal size and hurried from the beach into the jungle.

Hanuman had tangled with demons before and

worried that he might be recognized. So he again used his powers, this time changing his form to that of a black cat. He sped through the undergrowth until he came to the walls of the fortress.

He slunk up and over the parapet, the demon sentries barely paying him any mind. The vast compound provided plenty of shadows as he searched for Sita.

In time, he reached the very heart of the fortress: Ravana's palace. And there in the courtyard, he saw a beautiful woman tied to an ashoka tree. Around her a dozen armed demons stood guard. It could only be Sita. Satisfied, he slunk back to the beach, changed his form again, and leaped back to the mainland.

"She is there!" Hanuman called before his feet even alit on the beach.

"Well done," Rama said to him. "Now, can you carry us?"

Hanuman shrank back to his normal size. "No. My powers have limits. I cannot carry others. Besides, we need help. There are many, many *rakshasas* in the fortress, indeed all over the island."

"Rama and I have faced demons before," Lakshmana said.

"Of course," Hanuman said. "But not like these. And none like Ravana himself. We need an army."

Rama understood. "Fetch your people. We will go together, tear down the stronghold, and rescue Sita."

"But how will we get them all across?" Lakshmana said. "We have no boat even for ourselves."

Hanuman smiled as he grew tall again, preparing to make his leap. "I have a notion. While I am gone, gather stones. As many as you can find. Great ones and small ones."

"Stones?" Lakshmana was almost annoyed. "What good are ordinary stones against such enemies? They will only sink our boats—"

"Trust me!" Hanuman said as he launched himself north, back to the monkey kingdom, back to the army King Sugriva had promised them.

35

"So you see, Rama could not have done without Hanuman."

Nek picks up his cup, but his hand trembles, so Ram takes it for him and holds it to his lips. He knows the man needs to rest, but he cannot help saying, "But Rama was powerful. Surely he could have found a way."

Nek gulps, lies back with his eyes shut. "I suppose. But it is the way of things. No one is meant to be alone. No one is meant to never need help or friendship. Not even gods."

In seconds Nek's breathing evens out, and Ram knows he is asleep.

Ram's fingertips worry the grooves carved on the bead at his neck. He flips through the scenes from Rama's tale, calling each one up like a picture in his mind. Rama breaking the bow, winning Sita. Rama accepting his fate, embracing his exile in the forest though no one else wanted it. Jatayu glimpsing Ravana carrying Sita away. Sita cleverly dropping her jewels. And Hanuman. How wonderful that he appeared at the right moment, that he remembered who he was, what he had been born to do.

And Ram realizes that Nek is absolutely right. No one is meant to be alone. The truth of it gives him courage to do what he must.

Ram's idea grows and changes shape and form like Hanuman himself. He has to leave Nek. Singh will finish work in a few hours. The bullies will be back at nightfall. It is time.

Ram puts two more pills and some food within Nek's reach.

He tiptoes down the stairs. At the bottom, he fits the smaller key into the padlock securing the chain to Nek's bicycle. He wheels the bicycle out of the alley and onto the street.

He guides the bicycle, struggling more than once

with the turns. He wishes he knew how to ride it. Maybe when this is all over, Nek will teach him.

He stops once at a busy corner to rest, glancing down and cursing the bike for being so heavy. Something is etched on the top tube of the bicycle's frame, rust filling in the scratching. It is writing. Ram runs his finger over, feels the rough edges, wonders what it says. One of the words could be Nek's name, but he can't be sure.

It takes him almost an hour, sweating and sore, to push the bicycle back to the garden.

Sita waits in the slanting afternoon light. Ram must work quickly.

He leans the bicycle against a tree and hurries to mix some mortar.

All that remains is her face, and the veil.

The veil is easy. Ram already worked out how he'd attach it. He dabs a thin bead of mortar around her head, from jawline to jawline, just in front of where her ears would be.

Then he carefully lays the edge of the *dupatta*— the hemmed finished edge—along the line, cementing it into place. The folds of the veil fall perfectly, the mirrors licking up the golden light dappling through the trees.

Nek would be proud.

Now, her face.

Nek carved the long straight nose, etched out the full lips, and hollowed out the eye sockets when the concrete was still wet. But Sita is different from the warriors Ram has seen the artist make. Her eyes are deep, waiting for something to fill them in. The warrior statues have only small eyes, squinting in laughter, just slits in the cement.

He can't let Sita be seen like this.

Nek must have had a plan for what he would do for the eyes. There must be something under the tarp. Soon he finds a cigar box that rattles when he picks it up. He lifts the lid. Inside are stones— beautiful ones!—creamy colored, worn smooth as glass. *River stones*, Ram thinks, and wonders how he knows this. Perfect. He finds two of similar size, shaped like almonds. Then he packs the eye socket on the statue's face with a bit of cement and settles one stone gently in place. In a moment he has the other done as well.

Ram steps back, surveys his work. Better. But not quite.

Her eyes stare too blankly. He dips his little finger into the bucket of mortar and dabs a quick dot of cement in the middle of one creamy white stone eye. Yes. That's better. He has to do the left one twice, having placed the iris too far to the outside on the first go, but when he is finished, he is pleased.

She looks like a queen. Just like the real Sita. Like a work of art.

He'd like to give her eyes a chance to dry before he takes her out into the street, but he's running out of time. He readies the bicycle, lining the crate with burlap scraps so the bangle edges won't snag on the wood. Then he goes to lift Sita.

She's heavier than he thought. And his muscles feel loose, his legs wobbly when he manages to get her up in his arms. He moves deliberately, testing each leg before he trusts it, making his way to the bicycle. He struggles to lift Sita high enough to clear the rim of the crate. She drops unceremoniously, and Ram's heart pounds. Is she broken? But from what he can see, Sita is not only beautiful, but sturdy as well.

He pulls the bike to the road. The sky burns orange and pink. The light dances madly off the mirrors. She'll attract too much attention this way. Ram leans the bike against a tree, goes back and fetches another sack to drape over her head.

But in the clearing, he hears something. Voices.

Coming from Shiva's ridge.

Clutching the bag, Ram crouches and listens.

The voices have stopped speaking, but now he hears a sound like an elephant crashing down the path. Beams from two electric flashlights dance in the gloom.

No.

"Down here's a bunch of garbage, Uncle." Peach Fuzz's voice is unmistakable. "The rat stole it, you can be sure, just like he stole my new watch. I bet it is material from all the construction in town."

He's back already? He must have decided Ram wouldn't pay, or maybe just decided he'd rather make Ram pay by destroying the garden.

They draw closer. The man with him breathes heavily. "Slow down, Vijay. There is no hurry."

And then Ram glimpses the man's face. He is round and short, with eyebrows like the red-and-black crests of hoopoe birds.

Singh's commissioner.

Ram slinks out, silent as a panther.

He fetches the bicycle and Sita, pushing as fast as he can toward the noise of 22.

There is still hope. Maybe if Singh can give him

enough money, he can keep both the boy *and* his uncle quiet.

A few hundred yards from the path, halfway back to the sector, Ram steps onto a groomed bed of gravel. The road crew was busy today. The pavement has inched closer to the garden.

Soon it will pass by the garden. Soon more people will have reason to venture out here.

More people will discover the secret.

But he can't worry about them now. There is nothing he can do to stop the road. Only perhaps to buy Nek some time to figure out what to do next.

He has to find Singh.

36

By the time he reaches the shrine at the corner, his arms and legs are weak. His belly feels as empty as a tiffin at supper time, but he wishes harder for water, anything to drink. His throat is dry and rough—these cold nights lately, he guesses. But he doesn't dare stop.

The factory emits its usual noises and smells. As Ram passes the gate, the guard comes out to watch him.

"That's the trashman's bicycle."

Ram doesn't answer.

"What's that in the basket?"

Ram ignores him.

The dancing school lady is also in her doorway, seeing her students off. Ram catches her eye. She frowns, tilts her head to the side. Ram reaches up and pulls the cover a little higher over Sita's head.

A crew of street sweepers is hard at work, picking up torn paper, sweeping ash, the exploded shells from hundreds of fireworks. One of them notices Ram, speaks to the others. They laugh. Ram can't quite hear them. They seem oddly far away.

Rakesh is cleaning his pots. "Have you seen Singh uncle today?" Ram asks.

Rakesh makes a face. "Where did you get a bicycle?"

"From my friend," Ram says. "I borrowed it."

"I just saw Daya a minute ago. Sri Singh has not left yet."

"Thanks."

"Boy, you look terrible. Here—I have some leftovers—"

This might be the first time Rakesh has offered him anything for free. But Ram's belly clenches at the thought of food. He waves him off, continues walking. The bicycle is getting so heavy.

At the corner, Daya is bouncing a tennis ball

against the wall. "Ram!" She misses the ball when she sees him. "I've been worried about—"

"Is your father still here?"

Daya nods. She eyes the crate. "Is that—"

"Go get him, please."

Daya bolts up the steps, flinging open the door before the doorman has time to pull it for her. The doorman eyes Ram curiously.

Ram holds the bike steady as he kneels awkwardly next to it. *Why does my head seem to keep moving even when I am still?* he wonders.

The doorman opens the door, and Singh and Daya hurry down the steps.

"Ram, what's going on? Daya says you need help."

Ram swallows. "I have come to help you."

Singh smiles in surprise. "Oh?"

"You need art," Ram announces. "For your museum."

"Ram—"

Ram sways on his feet. "You like art. And you have money to spend?"

Singh holds an arm out ready to catch Ram should he fall. "What's going on?"

"Listen," Ram pleads. "You want the art to be

special. To be like India. To be real. Yes?" He practiced the words over and over in his head, but now
it is all he can do to even speak. But maybe Sita can
speak for him.

"Ram, are you all right? You look unwell."

Ram uses the frame of the bicycle like a crutch as
he lifts the burlap sack off Sita's head. "Look."

Singh is quiet, and Ram feels that for one brief
moment, the world has stopped spinning around
him. He peels back more of the sack, shoving what
he can down around the feet of the statue.

Singh's mouth hangs open slightly, his eyes wide
and shining like Sita's. "Did you make this, Ram?"

"I helped. My friend is a great artist. And you
said great art is costly. I will sell you this for your
museum."

Now that he has said it out loud, Ram hears how
feeble his plan is. He must convince Mr. Singh to
buy Sita and put her in a museum. He must get
a good enough price to supply Nek with enough
money to stay on in the city and send some to his
family. Enough money to give him time to find
another job if indeed he has been fired like the
guard said. And enough money to pay off that bully
and his important uncle.

But this is the only way. This *must* be the miracle. When he and Nek have more time, they can figure out what to do next, how to keep Nek from having to abandon his garden.

From having to abandon Ram.

Singh leans in and studies Sita's dress. "Bangles?" he whispers. "Electrical wire. And concrete?"

"His friend uses only rubbish to make beautiful art," Daya says.

Singh circles to the other side.

"You like it," Ram says.

Singh puts a hand on the top of his *dastar*. "I've never seen anything like it."

Ram hopes that is good.

"You have to buy it."

"Ram, I—"

Ram can't bear to hear what he fears is coming next. "We must have money or everything will be lost! I have to save them!"

"Them?" Singh asks.

Daya's voice is choked with tears. "I think he means the other statues, Papa."

"And Nek uncle. And his family." *And me,* Ram adds silently.

Singh speaks slowly, quietly. "Ram, this sculp-

ture is extraordinary. But I can't buy anything without the permission of the artist. I don't even have
any money to give you now. . . ."

He goes on and on. But all Ram hears is *can't,
won't, no.*

"Please," Ram says.

"Let's go see your friend. We can talk about it.
These things take time, Ram."

But there is no time. Peach Fuzz and his uncle
are there. Probably making plans about where to
direct the bulldozer first.

Ram has failed.

"This was a bad idea." He stumbles around to the
handlebar. How is it so much heavier than it was
earlier?

"Ram!" Singh says with alarm. "Wait—you—"

Ram pushes the bicycle back toward the garden.
He should return the statue before he goes back to
Nek. How will he tell his friend what is happening?
What is about to happen?

He considers Rama. Rama the hero. Rama always
did everything right, even when it was the wrong
thing. He left Ayodhya because he was a good son.
A son who happily obeyed his father's wishes. But if
he'd stayed, if he'd just said no, then Sita wouldn't

have gotten kidnapped by stupid Ravana.

Ram knows he is no hero. So if a hero does everything right even when it is wrong, maybe Ram can do something wrong because it is right.

He looks at Singh.

He'll do.

If the garden is going to be destroyed, Ram will make sure it is remembered.

"*Chalo.*" He leans into the handlebars. "I need to show you something, Uncle ji."

"*Chalo*," Ram repeats.

"Please, Papa," Daya says. "I know where he's going."

Singh hurries around to stand in front of the bike. "Ram," he says. "You are sick. Show us tomorrow."

Singh is probably right. Ram guesses he has caught whatever it was that Nek came back with. And lying down sounds like a very good idea. Ram is sure he would sleep as soon as he hit the ground.

But tomorrow is too late. Peach Fuzz and his uncle might have workmen there by morning. Even tonight, they could be kicking over statues, tearing up the ground.

"No," Ram says. "Now."

Singh rubs the hair at his neck below the band of the *dastar*. It is growing late. A few of the oil lamps have already been lit in the apartment and shop windows. "How far?" he asks Daya.

"Not far," she fibs. "A few minutes."

Singh sighs. "At least let me push the bicycle."

Ram surrenders it. Daya seizes his hand. Singh murmurs to the doorman, "Come with us, Anik? In case?"

Ram starts to protest. He's terrified to show Nek's garden even to Singh. But what choice does he have now? Maybe one more won't hurt.

And then they move again. Ram and Daya lead the way, followed by Singh as he wheels the bicycle bearing the magnificent Sita statue, uncovered now for all to see. Let them see. The more who know what Nek has done before it is gone, the better. The doorman brings up the rear of the column and they round the corner of the building, heading up Ram's street.

Rakesh is dropping the canvas awning he uses to cover the samosa stand during the day. "Rakesh uncle," Daya shouts. "Come with us!"

"Daya!" Ram's voice is weak. "No! Too many people!"

It is too late. Rakesh is already stepping out from under the canvas. He never could refuse Daya.

"Come where, princess? What's wrong with Ram?" He is still wearing his apron, the bib stained with oil, pockets jingling with the day's earnings.

"Who made that?" Rakesh asks.

"Ram," Singh says. "And his friend."

They are now a crowd of five, six if you count Sita riding in her palanquin.

The street sweepers scoop up the last pile of litter into the back of the truck parked by the roadside. One of them calls out to Rakesh. "Hey! No more parades!"

Ram ignores them. Thankfully, they don't follow. But when they pass the factory gates, the last of the workers straggle out, and the guard locks up the gate behind them.

"Isn't that Nek's bike?" one of the workers says.

"That kid went by with it earlier," the guard answers.

"What is that in the basket?" another asks.

"Nothing!" Ram manages. This isn't what he had in mind. Not at all. He doesn't want all these people to see. Nek certainly wouldn't. "It's nothing. Leave us alone!"

"Yeah!" Daya says. "Go away!"

Ram tries to walk faster, but his legs are feeling heavier with every step. And despite his pleas, one of the factory men has joined them, talking quietly with Rakesh.

They are a proper procession now, trailing down the block, halfway to the corner with the shrine. The dancing school lady watches from her doorway, but thankfully, she doesn't follow.

By the time they pass the shrine, two people Ram doesn't even know have joined the parade. Ram hesitates.

"This isn't how it was supposed to go, Daya."

She squeezes his hand. "I'm sorry, Ram. Should we go back? Tell me what to do."

Ram doesn't know what to do himself. And they've come this far. They've seen Sita. He doesn't see another option.

"*Chalo.*"

They wrap around the corner, step off the sidewalk onto the gravel for the new road.

At least no one else joins them before they reach the path that cuts into the forest.

"Here," Daya says. "This way."

The rosewood leaves *shush-shush* overhead. Acacia pods crunch under their feet. The monkeys have gone silent. They work their way up the path into the clearing.

"Ram, we need light," Daya says.

Ram's arm feels wobbly when he points at the supply tarp. "In there."

Soon a flashlight switches on, and then the torch is lit. As the light grows, Ram wonders what he could have been thinking. They don't belong here. All of them in this space feels wrong.

But what choice does he have?

"Is this what you want us to see, Ram? Where Sita was made?"

Ram kneels down. He's brought them this far. He should be the one to show them. But he's so tired.

"Show them, Daya."

"But Ram—"

"Please." Ram looks at her. "You remember the places?"

She nods. "I remember."

"Ram, are you sure this can't wait until tomorrow?" Singh pleads.

"Please, Uncle ji."

They shuffle off, leaving Ram alone. He lies back, closes his eyes, tries to imagine how he will tell Nek what a mess he has made of things.

He's not sure how long the others are gone, but when he hears voices, he opens his eyes to see lights coming back up the path.

Ram props himself up on one arm.

Daya rushes to Ram's side. "I showed them. They seemed to like it. Now what?"

Ram has no idea.

The others trickle back. Rakesh and the doorman come, talking in low voices and stealing glances at Ram. Then the other worker and the stranger who joined them because he had nothing better to do. He hears Nek's name mentioned once or twice but cannot understand what they are saying.

Then Peach Fuzz appears. He's been here the whole time? He and his uncle must have explored further. Peach Fuzz looks so unhappy and annoyed that Ram feels a smile creep onto his face.

But he doesn't have time to savor the small victory. Singh and the commissioner enter the clearing, speaking quietly. The commissioner shoots Ram odd glances from beneath his hoopoe-bird brows. Ram has no idea what any of it means.

Maybe it means nothing. Maybe they think he's as crazy as Ram thought Nek was when he first came. Whatever they are saying, Ram can't do anything about it now. Everything he could do is done. He leans against Daya and shuts his eyes and lets sleep wash over him at last.

38

In the two days it took Hanuman to hasten home and collect the monkey army, Rama and Lakshmana built a mountain of stones on the beach. There was not so much as a loose pebble for miles in any direction.

When the monkeys finally marched from the jungle onto the clean yellow sand, each warrior, great and small, carried boulders *they* had collected on their journey.

They wasted no time.

The first wave of soldiers marched into the sea, dropped their stones in a great pile, and then waded back to collect more. The second wave of monkeys then marched out, dropped their stones on top of the first bunch, and then they turned back for more. As if by magic, the stone road across the sea grew. Stone by stone, they drew nearer and nearer to Sita. The monkeys, so full of chatter, were silent as they worked, tails and bearded chins held high and proud.

Finally the mountain of rock on the beach was picked clean, and the road stretched straight and true to the shore of Lanka.

Now the monkey army fell in behind Hanuman, who stepped behind Rama and Lakshmana. The two brothers readied their weapons, glanced once at each other and then to the great army assembled behind them. Then they sprinted over the stone bridge.

When they reached the shore, they kept right on running, up the sand and through the jungle. Here the monkeys took to the trees, swinging alongside and ahead of Rama and Lakshmana. They crashed upon the fortress walls like a storm, swarming over and through and around to face the enemy.

The monkeys fought fiercely—tooth and tail, club

and claw—swarming over the legions of *rakshasas*. Many of Hanuman's warriors fell.

Rama and Lakshmana fought side by side. The swath around them widened as they cut through the guards and breached the fortress walls. Their blades sang. Their arrows rained. Rama's golden discus zipped in and out of the horde, felling hundreds of Ravana's warriors.

Abruptly the demons fell back to the heart of the fortress, Ravana's palace, as if pulled by some silent command.

The monkeys chittered and screeched, hopping up and down as they celebrated what appeared to be a victory.

"Wait!" Rama cried.

From the palace emerged a great and terrible warrior. He carried a double-edged sword as tall as a man. His red eyes rolled about, and the monkeys scurried behind Rama, Lakshmana, and Hanuman.

But this demon had only two arms—two arms like pythons after swallowing deer, but only two arms, nonetheless.

It was not Ravana.

The demon roared out a challenge, dared anyone to come forward to face him.

Lakshmana did not hesitate.

Lifting his own sword, he rushed forward, swift as an eagle diving. The demon swung, but he was slow, his eyes betraying his movements before he made them. Lakshmana ducked the blow, spun inside the monster's reach, and jabbed with his sword.

The demon fell, puffed into a cloud of red dust, and disappeared before the other *rakshasas* even realized their champion was no more.

But one of the demons instantly understood.

A roar thundered down on the assembled army, and a new figure appeared atop the walls surrounding the palace.

All twenty of Ravana's eyes focused on Rama. His twenty hands clutched an arsenal of wicked weapons. Even his own *rakshasas* cowered.

Lakshmana returned to his brother's side. They did not have to speak to understand each other. Lakshmana placed a hand on his brother's shoulder in blessing and then went to stand with Hanuman.

Ravana bounded down from the wall and flew at Rama.

From the first stroke, both Rama and Ravana understood how well matched they were. They met blow for blow, strength for strength. Ravana knew god or demon could not hurt him, so how did this upstart mortal manage to withstand him? And Rama knew that it was for this moment that the holy man had trained him. It was for this moment that his own path had led him into exile. Perhaps even for this very moment that he had been born.

Along with his terrible weapons, Ravana wielded powerful magic, casting curses at Rama. But Rama was unafraid. He had learned well, and his heart was pure, so he parried every curse with the good magic he had learned from the holy man and deflected the evil.

Finally Ravana had used every weapon he possessed. They lay broken and useless around him. He had exhausted every ounce of bad magic he could muster.

Yet Rama still stood before him.

And Rama had a single arrow remaining.

He prayed, nocked the arrow, and launched it high into the heavens. Its song whistled clear and bright and sent all the other demons to the ground, clutching their ears in pain. As it arced past the sun and bent back to earth, it picked up speed, homing straight for Ravana. The demon king tried to run, but the arrow followed him, picking up speed as it drew nearer and nearer.

The arrow pierced Ravana's belly, right at the navel, and the fearsome demon king burst into flame.

The light was so great that all the demons scattered at once. They knew their time had ended. Their king had fallen. The fireball bloomed bright and intense for a second more before it consumed itself and vanished.

The quiet held a second longer before the monkey army erupted in celebration. The throng around Rama and Lakshmana danced and shouted and screeched wildly.

They were so joyous and noisy that for a moment

Rama didn't hear the voice calling to him.

But then he saw Sita standing in the gate of the ruined palace. And he smiled. He broke free, ran toward her, and embraced her at last.

Two days pass. Someone feeds Ram, gives him water, but his eyes won't focus and his tongue won't cooperate and he drops off before he can make sense of where he is or what has happened.

His adventures of the last few weeks muddle together with Rama's in his dreams. The monkey army. The statues. The bridge. The jungle. The battle. Shiva's bow and Shiva's head. Ravana's defeat. He is half-aware of someone telling him the story, but he slips in and out of sleep so freely that it all gets mixed together.

On the third day, he wakes to familiar voices. Gray light washes through a single window.

Nek's room, Ram realizes. He is at Nek's. But how? He struggles to sit up, pushing up against the cotton pallet he's been laid on, the blankets tangling around his arms.

"Hey, Papa!"

Daya? And Singh?

"How did I get here?"

Nek sits in the chair where Ram had camped before.

"We brought you," Singh says, relief flooding his voice. "You were very sick."

"You caught my fever," Nek says.

Ram looks at Daya. "Do you have it now?"

She shakes her head. "Papa took you to the doctor. They knew what medicine you needed and gave me something to keep me from getting so sick. I only threw up once," she says proudly.

"But how did you find Nek uncle? I never told you where he lives."

Daya smiles. "His name and address are etched on the frame of the bike. Right along the top tube."

Ram remembers the writing there. "Oh."

"Once we could see you were going to be all right, it was easy enough to find Nekji," Singh explains.

Now Ram understands that if they are all here together, Singh and Daya will have told Nek what he did. How he led those people to the garden.

He cannot look at Nek. He can't quite figure out how to ask the question. "Is Sita all right?"

"Sita is fine."

Ram finally meets Nek's eyes. "I didn't know what else to do."

"I know."

Ram waits for him to say more. Waits for Nek to tell him it was a stupid idea, or that he should have asked Nek first. "I thought if I could get him to buy her for the museum, then it would be enough money to pay off the gang. Enough for you to stay. That you could still take care of Ayushee and Vinod and still stay in Chandigarh and keep working on the garden. But then that boy and his uncle showed up so early and Singh uncle said no and I—"

"Stop babbling, Ram," Daya says. "Can I tell him?" she asks Singh and Nek.

Both nod.

"That bully's uncle. He's Papa's boss."

Ram's eyes study the pattern on the quilt. "I recognized him."

"And Nek uncle has been fired from the factory."

Tears prick hot and angry at Ram's eyes. But Nek and Singh are still smiling.

What is going on?

"And Nek uncle won't sell any of the statues," Daya continues.

"But—"

"Really, Ram!" Daya is properly annoyed now. "If you keep interrupting, I won't be able to finish."

Nek laughs. Singh clucks at Daya.

"That commissioner liked Nek's statues. Vijay was so mad! You should have seen it, Ram. It was wonderful!"

"He liked them? Your commissioner?"

"Of course he liked them, dummy!" Daya says. "Everyone liked them. Rakeshji, Anikji . . . all of them. And everyone else who's been there since likes them too."

"Everyone else?" Ram's voice is small. More people have come? He glances at Nek, but the man's expression is unreadable.

"Some of the city people are really mad. That forest is city property. They were going to finish the street and build a new sector next year. They called Nek uncle a—" She pauses, looks to her father. "What did they call him, Papa?"

"A thieving upstart," Singh and Nek say in chorus.

"But some of them say Nek uncle is a genius.

They like all the statues so much that they want the garden to stay! They want it to be a park so everybody in town will want to come and see. Maybe even everybody in all of India!"

Ram can't believe it.

Nek can't sit quietly any longer. "They are too hopeful."

"It appears your friend may soon have a new job, Ram," Singh says. "As an artist."

An artist! "Do artists get paid more than factory workers?"

"But it is more than just money!" Daya is bouncing up and down. "Workers to help him, and trucks to bring the rubbish from around the city so he doesn't have to haul it on his bicycle."

Ram is too shocked to speak, to even smile.

He'd *failed*. It had all gone so wrong. And now this?

It is more fantastic and magical than anything out of Rama's tale.

Singh places a hand on Daya's shoulder. "We should go, Daya," he says. "Ram needs to rest."

"He's been resting for *three* days," she says.

"Daya." Singh's voice is quiet. "They need to talk."

"*Acha.*" Daya climbs up off the floor. "I don't

have to go back to school until next week. So hurry up and get better. There are lots of kids out in the park during break. Easy pickings."

"Daya!" Singh's voice is sharper now.

Ram can't help smiling now. Daya flicks her braids and goes to the door as Singh and Nek shake hands.

When Daya and Singh have gone, Ram sees that Nek is holding something.

Ram's bead. Still strung on the loop of red cord he usually wears around his neck. They must have taken it off him when he slept.

"Sri Singh asked if I was the one who made it."

Ram fights the urge to snatch it from Nek's hand as his face flushes hot with embarrassment. How many times had he hoped the same thing?

"What did you tell him?"

"That I didn't."

And even though Ram had thought the idea stupid himself, it still hurts to have the possibility—however slim—struck down. "I didn't say you did."

"It would have made a great story, though," Nek says. "To find out we were somehow linked because of this little piece of art."

Ram wipes his eyes.

"She gave it to you, didn't she?" Nek asks. "The girl?"

Ram's chest tightens. "She isn't coming back, is she?"

Nek waits a long time before speaking. "She would have if she could, Ram. I know it."

"I won't ever find her, will I?"

Nek does not answer for a long time. "I'm sorry, Ram. I know what it means to lose someone. I know how that kind of hope hurts." Ram nods. He remembers how sad Nek was when he spoke of the sister he lost when his family left Pakistan.

"Why didn't you show me before?"

Ram struggles to find the words. "It's stupid. I thought . . . When you started telling me about Rama and how he was secretly Vishnu . . . maybe I was secretly . . . *somebody* instead of a nobody with no family."

Nek doesn't ask him to finish. Ram blinks hard.

After a beat, Nek speaks. "You were somebody to Pehn." Nek leans forward and puts the bead in Ram's hand. "And you are somebody to me."

Ram can't speak.

"Besides, Vinod is much too small to work for me yet, so you will have to do."

Ram wipes his eyes, sniffs noisily.

Nek pats his shoulder.

Finally Ram manages to speak. "A happy ending," he manages. "Just like Rama's and Sita's."

"But you don't know the ending yet," Nek says.

Ram sits up. "You told me," he realizes. "As I slept. Rama defeated Ravana. He and Sita were reunited."

Nek smiles. "That's the *victory*. We celebrate the victory at Dussehra. But it is not the end. The end is what we celebrate at Diwali. The *most* important part of the story."

"What's more important than defeating Ravana and rescuing Sita?"

Nek swallows, blinks twice before he speaks. "Finding home."

40

S ita, Rama, Lakshmana, and Hanuman left Lanka. The monkey army raced ahead, heralding the victory. As word of the death of the demon king traveled throughout the jungle, the birds and animals gathered to salute the victors on their return journey. And when the news reached the towns and villages, they, too, came out to see the heroes, showering them with flowers and gifts and food, eager for a glimpse of beautiful Sita and the mighty trio of warriors.

When at last they arrived at Mount Rishyamukha, they feasted and celebrated for weeks with the monkey kingdom. But after a while, Lakshmana pulled his brother aside.

"It is time for us to go home."

"Why rush back to our hut in the jungle? We have friends here now."

"No!" Lakshmana smiled. "*Home.* The fourteen years have ended. We can go back to Ayodhya."

And Rama realized, with all the many adventures, and now with his joy at rescuing Sita, he had lost track of the days and months they'd been away. "Can it be?"

"Yes," Lakshmana replied. "Are you ready to be king?"

"I am ready to do my duty," he replied.

King Sugriva was sad to lose his new friends, and even sadder when Hanuman decided to make the journey with them. But in his gratitude, he gave them a great chariot and swift horses to ease their journey north.

Eager now to see Ayodhya again, the foursome traveled swiftly, even at night. Still, the animals lined the way through the wilderness, and as they passed the settlements and other kingdoms, the people all rushed out to see them. At dusk and through the darkness, their admirers bore oil lamps to show the way.

Soon the whole country had heard of the wonderful victory of Rama over Ravana, of the light over the darkness. And in addition to coming out to pay honor to the heroes, they lit even more lamps, the light itself paying tribute. Millions of tiny clay oil lamps carpeted the countryside, floated along the great rivers, dotted the plains like a blanket of stars, and climbed up the slopes of the foothills.

The lights led all the way back to Ayodhya. When Rama, Lakshmana, Sita, and Hanuman drew within sight of the kingdom, it was clear that they, too, had heard about the victory and the coming return of their true king. The entire city had been polished clean. Oil lamps glittered from every window, atop every wall, along every path.

And so it was that Rama followed the lights back home. After fourteen long years in exile, after a great many adventures, after making many new friends and ridding the world of terrible enemies, Rama was finally back in the place he belonged.

ONE YEAR LATER

Festival season has come again. Worshippers carry a Ganesha idol on their shoulders as they make their way up the lane. Ram pedals the bike through the traffic circle with Daya perched on the handlebars. He reaches up to loosen his tie, fingers checking the cord and the beads. Nek made him a new one to hang beside Pehn's. He's let her go, but he still wears the bead, only now in memory instead of hope of finding her. It aches, that understanding that she really is gone. It grabs at his heart when he least expects it.

But having other family makes the sadness bearable.

His books and empty lunch tiffin rattle in the wire basket on the back of the bike as he rides. Ayushee is a much better cook than Nek. Lunch is easily the best part of Ram's school day, though playing in the yard during recess is all right too. The other kids still sneer at him because he is so behind, but they tolerate him because he is so good at games. They like him a lot better when he isn't winning their pocket money. And Ram tolerates the lessons well enough, even though there are not enough stories and too many exercises to write out. But he figures that if Rama could last fourteen years in exile, he can get through a few hours of school every day. And like Rama, he doesn't have to endure it alone. Daya, Ram was surprised to learn, is as feared and respected as kids twice her size and age. So it's almost better than having Lakshmana at his side. Even Vijay leaves him alone now.

He slows down long enough for Daya to spring off the handlebars when they arrive at her father's building.

"I'll ask Papa if I can come today!" She bounds up the stairs.

"Should I wait?" Ram asks, checking his watch. This one is different. A solid old metal one that he winds every night. Singh found it and had it refurbished for Ram's birthday this year. It keeps perfect time.

"*Nahi*," Daya says as Anik opens the door for her, waving at Ram. "We'll come when we can."

Ram pushes off, rounds the corner.

He rings his bell as he passes Rakesh, who lifts the metal tongs in salute. The guard at the factory nods as he passes.

He makes a tight turn around the corner by the shrine.

The new road is finished. The dirt and gravel chasm between what used to be the end of the city and the forest is gone. A few new buildings have sprung up, but the trees and vines hang as lush and thick as before. The parking area is almost done, but Ram still favors his old paths. He won't be able to use them much longer. The walls enclosing the edges of the garden are coming along quickly now that Nek has so many men to carry out his plans.

They've widened the path from the road into the forest, but the tall rosewood still marks the way, branches arcing over the path, the leaves whispering a welcome now instead of the warning they once did. Ram rides under the branches and into the forest. The old tarp and jumble of supplies have been replaced by a stout workshop and even a little office for Nek. In the dirt outside, a pretty woman crouches, passing a ball of yarn with a chubby little boy, drool shining on his chin.

"Where is he?" Ram dismounts. He sheds his school blazer, kicks off his shoes, and peels off his socks. Of all the changes over the last year, wearing shoes and socks has been the hardest one to adjust to.

"You have to change clothes before you go to help him." Ayushee tries to sound firm, but she isn't very good at it.

"I won't get too dirty, Auntie ji," Ram promises.

Ayushee scoops up Vinod. "He's up with Shiva. They've been waiting for you."

Ram rubs the top of Vinod's head and takes off.

The path is paved now, and Ram knows the way well enough. He should. He helped lay the stone. When he reaches the spot, he stops. The walls run canyon high on both sides, sculpted out of cement and the burlap sacks the cement came in. They ripple down to a stream that meanders by in lazy curves. Above the stream stands a set of figures, water jugs balanced on their heads. Even higher up, Lord Shiva stands vigil.

"Where have you been, slowpoke?" Nek calls down. "We are almost ready!"

Ram climbs up to where Nek and two of his men wait. They are muddy but smiling.

"Is it done?" Ram asks.

Nek calls down to someone on the other side at the bottom of the slope. "Now!"

The man at the bottom pulls a cord that starts the pump. Ram can hear the chuffing of the motor faintly, but a whooping and gurgling sound as well, and then the water begins to flow from where they stand. It cascades from mighty Shiva's feet, pours over the edge, and plummets down. Soon it runs steadily, the water flowing ceaselessly, filling the jars of the water bearers below and running off into the stream, then being pumped back up to the top to make the circuit again.

The workers cheer. Nek places a hand on Ram's shoulder and squeezes gently.

"Just like you imagined," Ram says to him.

"Better."

જ ભ

AUTHOR'S NOTE

A book is never just one idea. I've heard other writers talk about how the blending and crashing of big ideas creates the story. This story is fictional but has deep roots in two very real stories. I feel ridiculously fortunate that both were rich with possibility.

I lived in Chandigarh, India, in 2005. One of the first places my new friends showed me was Nek Chand's Rock Garden in what is now Sector 1. Like many visitors to this wonderful place, I was amazed. The way Chand repurposed cast-off materials inspired me. The sheer volume and scale of his work humbled me. And the fact that he worked in secret on the garden for almost twenty years intrigued me. My family and I visited the garden again in 2009 when we returned to India to adopt our son. I knew then that I wanted to write this book to learn more about Nek Chand, the need we all have to create, and the magical mingling of story, art, and the world around us.

The *Ramayana* itself is a great example of this mingling. First written in Sanskrit in the fourth century BC, it tells the story of Rama, his triumph over Ravana, and his return home. I used to teach selections from it in my high school world literature classes, and I've read many of Hanuman's adventures to my own children. There are hundreds of versions of the *Ramayana*, all filled with dizzying detail. The version Ram hears in this book is very streamlined. I allowed myself the luxury of curating and winnowing it down to fit this book and parallel Ram's story.

I left out and modified a great deal of both Nek's story and the *Ramayana*. I encourage you to learn more about the Rock Garden and the real Nek Chand. Begin with the Nek Chand Foundation website (nekchand.com) for information about the artist and his work. To dive deeper into the *Ramayana*, consider R. K. Narayan's *The Ramayana: A Shortened Modern Prose Version of the Indian Epic.*

Even though I had to give up many wonderful details, Ram showed up very early and quickly claimed this story as his own. He came from many places. He grew out of my own experience of being an outsider in a culture as rich as India's. He grew out of imagining stories behind the lives of children in India without homes or families to look after them. And he grew out of wanting to write about the new story that is written when a child and a parent find each other.

As Nek says in this story, sometimes the made-up stories are the truest ones. I hope and believe he is right.

GLOSSARY

acha: okay

auntie: a term of respect for a woman older than
the speaker

bewakoof: dummy or fool

chai: tea made with milk, sugar, and spices

chalo: Hindi word meaning "Let's go."

changa: okay

changa fer?: Good, then?

dastar: a turban worn by a Sikh man

Diwali: The Hindu festival of lights. It is widely
observed across religions in India, celebrating
the triumph of good over evil. It also coincides
with the Sikh festival of Bandi Chhor Divas.

Dussehra: Festival celebrating Rama's victory over Ravana. It features parades, reenactments of the *Ramayana*, and the burning of giant straw-filled papier-mâché effigies of Ravana and his minions.

han/han ji: phrase meaning "yes"

harmonium: a freestanding keyboard instrument, played like a piano but relying on reeds to produce the sound

Hindu: a catchall term denoting the many indigenous religions in India

hoye: oh my

ji: a suffix showing respect

kheer: traditional rice pudding dessert

marg: road or path

naan: leavened bread traditionally cooked in a tandoor

nahi: no

neem: Tree whose leaves and oils are used for medicinal purposes. People have long used peeled branches to clean their teeth.

oh teri deri: expression of dismay

oye: wow, whoa, or cool

pagal: crazy, or nuts

paisa: 1/100 of a rupee

pakoras: chunks of vegetables, meat, or cheese,

dipped in chickpea flour batter and then
deep-fried

panga: "Taking a panga" means asking for trouble.

paratha: flatbread

Punjab: region of northern India and eastern
Pakistan

rangoli: Folk art patterns made on floors of homes
to celebrate festivals and welcome Hindu gods.
Rangoli are often made with colored rice, flour,
grains, or flower petals.

rickshaw: A sort of taxi used to transport people
around. Cycle rickshaws are pulled by bicycles.

roti: bread

rupee: basic unit of Indian currency

samosa: A stuffed, deep-fried pastry. Samosas
are often filled with some combination of
spices, vegetables, potatoes, and ground meat.

sari: long strip of unstitched cloth serving as a
garment for Indian women

shukriya: thank you

Sikh: follower of Sikhism, a faith widely practiced,
particularly in the Punjab area of India

siyappa: "drat" or "shoot"

tandoor: a traditional clay oven, often heated by a
wood fire

theek hai: all right or fine

tiffin: light lunch or container used for carrying a
light lunch

tuk-tuk: an auto rickshaw

uncle: a term of respect for an older man

wah ji wah: expression of awe

wallah: Hindi word that can mean a maker of
something or deliverer of something

ACKNOWLEDGMENTS

As ever, many thanks to Caitlyn Dlouhy for her generosity, patience, and vision. I am thrilled to have a book that not only bears the mark of your green pen but also your name. Thanks to the entire team at Atheneum Books for Young Readers who make stories into real live books. Thanks to Robin Rue and Beth Miller for their encouragement, friendship, and faith in my stories. Thanks to family and friends who motivate me and tolerate me in equal measure, but love me even more. Thanks to early readers of this book in its various forms—Julia Mesplay, Josiah Vellegas, and Stephanie Guerra—your keen eyes and honest reactions helped tremendously.

I am indebted to Ibadat Sahney for her guidance in language and customs. Thanks also go out to Neera, Vinod, Vineeta, Ayushee, and all my Bhavan Vidyalaya friends who welcomed me to Chandigarh and made sure I learned about Nek Chand's marvelous work. And thanks to Jim, Evie, and Arun, for reminding me every day of the joy of making the most of what we have.